KRISTA BECKWITH

Family Ties

First published by Success Press 2023

Copyright © 2023 by Krista Beckwith

This novel is entirely a work of fiction. The names, characters and incidents portrayed in it are the work of the author's imagination. Any resemblance to actual persons, living or dead, events or localities is entirely coincidental.

Krista Beckwith asserts the moral right to be identified as the author of this work.

Cover designed by: GetCovers

First edition

ISBN: 9782989804930

This book was professionally typeset on Reedsy.
Find out more at reedsy.com

Contents

Acknowledgement

I would like to thank my kids, my three heartbeats, for always supporting me. This story would probably still be in my mind if it weren't for y'all. I wanted to show you that it doesn't matter how old you are, it's never too late to pursue your dreams. A special thanks to my parents for being my beta readers, even if this was your first time reading a book in years! LOL! I'd also like to thank my other beta readers: Jaz, Hykiem and Mike. Thank each of you for your input on helping me improve this story. A huge thanks goes out to my sister and brother for always supporting me, no matter how much I get on your nerves and to YOU, the reader. Thank you for taking the time to read this book!

Chapter 1

Janelle

"Janelle, I wish my life was as perfect as yours! Girl, you've got the husband, the house and now the baby," exclaims my coworker Raquel as I told her the news of my pregnancy. "You literally are living the fairy tale life that every little girl only dreams of."

I take a moment to consider how my life must look to people outside, looking in. "You know, I can almost guarantee if we were to switch places you'd prefer yours over mine," I smile with a small chuckle. "I dead ass thought there was something wrong with me for the longest. It seemed as if death had taken everyone I ever loved from me. I mean, I'm already an only child *as well as* an only grandchild on both sides of my family. That made my dad's death at seven years old and my mom's death at eighteen absolutely devastating."

I take a sip of my tea as I blink away tears of sadness while hoping not to have hindered my grieving progress by bringing all that up. My mind has always associated loneliness with myself. As an only child I created an imaginary sister out of loneliness, experienced my first heartbreak from death by age seven and by eighteen, I was completely alone in this big world. I lost the two people I loved most. Shortly after, it was my grandparents' turn to see those pearly gates.

But Percy, my high school friend turned lover, has been a constant in my life since we reconnected at our ten-year high school reunion. It felt nice to finally have someone to love and who loves me back. I can't lie, I was totally smitten with him in high school, but he left for a full ride to a university for football while I decided to stay in Fairfield. Then after graduation, we dispersed our separate ways.

I can still remember the butterflies I felt when I laid eyes on him again at the reunion. My stomach clenched tightly, and I felt somewhat dizzy as he wrapped me in his warm embrace. We picked right back up where we left off and eventually grew to become more than friends. We were inseparable and went on to marry only a year after the reunion.

"Umm... HELLO??" Raquel nearly shouts as she snaps her fingers in front of my face, pulling me out of my thoughts. "I'm sorry, I didn't mean to bring up any tough memories for you. I just can't wait for my happily ever after."

I shake off my memories as we head back to our desks from the break room. "My bad, I just still have a hard time worrying that people I grow close to will end up dying unexpectedly. Now that I think about it, I should probably get back into therapy for this, but chile, this job and these measly benefits ain't gone cut it." We laugh as we sit down and place our headsets back on our heads.

"I can only hope that this pregnancy—", I'm cut off by an incoming call.

"9-1-1, what's your emergency?" I answer.

A panicked voice screams into the phone "There's been an accident along Highway 31, just past the city limits sign. It's a gray Dodge truck with one of those big spotlights on top."

My heart skips a beat for a second.

My husband Percy drives a Dodge Ram with a spotlight on top.

I dismiss the thought, it's not like he's the only person in Fairfield, South Carolina in a Dodge with a spotlight on his truck. I calmly ask "Is there anyone in the vehicle?"

The female voice replies " Yes, there's an unconscious man in the driver's side and there was a woman but she ran off before I had a chance to fully stop and get out of my car. I called out for her but she must be long gone, probably in shock because I didn't see her anywhere."

"I've dispatched emergency personnel to the location, they should arrive within the next three minutes. Can you tell if the driver is breathing?"

"I checked prior to calling but I didn't feel a pulse," the female caller replies. "Oh Lord, please don't let this man be dead. Jesus, please heal this man! Come wrap your arms around him and the woman for that matter and breathe life back into them. I ask you to heal them in your son Jesus' name, Amen. Amen. Amen!" the woman prays aloud.

She must be one of those highly religious people that attends church weekly and wears nothing but dresses or skirts. How do people have such blind faith in someone they've never even seen? *Does she really think God will save him?* I wonder to myself as I hear faint sirens coming from her end of the line.

"Oh! They're here!" she says. I hear her muffled voice yelling to gain the attention of the EMTs as she sets the phone down.

I don't disconnect the line until I hear emergency personnel in the background. Someone says "Do we have an ID?"

"A partial. His uniform badge says Officer Williams", another person replies.

I gasp as my heart quickens at the mention of the name Williams.

Wait! Officer Williams!? No! It can't be! Not Officer Percy Williams! Not MY Officer Percy Williams!

I instinctively disconnect the line and throw myself into 'Not Ready' to prevent any more calls from coming through. Grabbing my cell phone from my back pocket, I find Percy's name in my Favorites and press call.

Ring, ring, ring, ring..." After the fourth ring, it goes to voicemail. I hear Percy's deep, masculine voice, "I'm sorry I've missed your call. Please leave a message and I will get back to you as soon as possible."

"Babe, call me back ASAP! I need to know you're okay. There was a wreck with an Officer Williams in a gray Dodge truck with a spotlight. Call me!" I plead into the phone, "I love you so much, please tell me everything is okay."

Maybe I'm just overthinking, I think. After all, Percy did tell me that

4

he had to work late due to being short staffed. Correctional facility wardens can't just leave when their shift is up. They have to make sure there's proper coverage for inmates.

Yeah, I'm just overthinking as usual. Percy's fine.

* * *

I watch, my heart crumbling into a million shattered pieces, as the grave diggers slowly lower Percy's casket into the ground. Mascara stained tears line my face as I say my final goodbye to my husband. A distressed wail leaves my body as I try to stand from my seat. Without much to eat in the five days since his passing, I'm lightheaded just from sitting up. Once again, the person I loved the most has been taken from me.

Raquel and my best friend Harmony help me from my seat. I turn to hug the two of them but more so to balance myself and not fall to the ground. Grief slams into me like a semi truck as I experience the suffocating feeling that I've grown way too accustomed to.

"Take your time, Hun. We can stay however long you need", says Harmony with understanding eyes as she rubs a hand along my back.

I glance at her with puffy, swollen, red eyes while hoping they convey gratefulness for her and Raquel.

Raquel and I met 10 years ago at the first call center I worked at. She trained me, took me out for alcoholic drinks on our lunch break and has been stuck with me ever since. I didn't last long at that job because

I couldn't deal with the angry customers calling in wanting my help but cussing me out at the same time.

Harmony, on the other hand, is more like my sister from another mister. We go way back to our childhood years.

"You've gotta get some food in you though", protests Raquel. "When *was* the last time you ate anything?"

I think for a minute, "I don't know. I think it was like two days ago but I've had a few sips of water."

"You're gonna eat even if I have to feed you myself Janelle! You *have* to eat. It's not only you that you have to worry about. You're pregnant, we need you strong and the baby strong so you will always have a piece of Percy with you."

Truth be told, I can't even think about a future without Percy. I feel nothing but emptiness. My future seems dark, like a sunken place that I won't ever be able to escape from.

I nod, acknowledging my need to eat if not for myself, then for the baby.

"Isn't that Percy's coworker that's walking up?" asks Harmony with uncertainty.

I turn to glance over my shoulder just as Correctional Officer Anthony Miller reaches us.

"Janelle, I just wanted to personally come speak to you and give you my sincerest condolences," he states. "Percy was a great man and will be deeply missed. I just want to let you know that if you ever need anything...", he searches my eyes for understanding "and I do mean *anything*, please let me know."

He pulls me close for a hug. It's an endearing, warm embrace I didn't know I needed. For some reason, his touch felt like pure comfort and safety. Something I found in Percy but was once again swiftly ripped away from me.

"Thank you Anthony, it's appreciated", I reply as we loosen our hold and go our separate ways.

I look back once more at the grave of my husband before turning to walk towards the car with Raquel and Harmony alongside me.

A woman with striking similarities to me catches my eye off to the corner of the cemetery. We're about the same skin tone and height however she's a bit older with a cast on her right arm. She's dressed in all black everything, dress, shoes, hat and veil.

Harmony, Raquel and I get in the car to leave but before we do, I turn back to take another look at the woman. She's now at my husband's graveside.

Who the hell is this woman and how does she know my husband?

Chapter 2

Janelle - Four Months Later

I t's a late, crisp September morning. The sun shines harshly on my face between a slit in my dark black out curtains. It's been four months since Percy died and every single day feels more insufferable than the last. Somehow I've managed to maintain a healthy pregnancy although at times, this unborn child feels like a parasite languidly draining me of my nutrients, my body *and* my beauty.

I found out through an early blood test that I'm having a precious little girl. I haven't really had time to think of names because of being so overwhelmed with everything. I found out around the time I was busy making funeral arrangements for Percy, so I haven't even had a chance to be excited about my little girl.

I'm not prepared for this day or any day for that matter but I promised Harmony I would allow her to get me out of the house. I eventually make my way out of bed and to the bathroom for a shower. As of late, I've been showering in the dark with only the sunlight from the bathroom window beaming against the decorative privacy film. Its pattern tends to give me a nostalgic feeling of childhood as rays of rainbow paint the shower walls. However, today I actually want to look somewhat decent although I know I may never feel that way again.

I flip on the light switch, shunning my eyes as they adjust to the bright lights filling the room. I take one look in the mirror and nearly shit myself! I look like death rolled over three times.

Damn, I've really let myself go since Percy left me.

My hair, although loc'd, is in a matted mess. They have started bonding with other locs, if I don't do something about this I'll end up with those 'Florida Boy' style wick locs. My new growth is ridiculous, my eyes and cheeks are sunken and I look like I stank.

I strip myself of my nightshirt and panties after turning on the water as hot as I can stand it then I hop in. The water burns my skin but I don't mind. I need a steaming hot, thorough shower to get all this funk off of me.

Once that's done, I lather myself up in some raspberry and bergamot lotion then start separating my locs and retwisting it while playing some old school R&B music on my Bluetooth speaker. It takes about an hour to finish my entire head but luckily I woke up with enough time to retwist them and let them air dry somewhat.

I walk over to my closet to figure out what to wear. I eventually decide on jeans and a casual mustard yellow blouse and head back to the bathroom to apply some light makeup.

Just as I'm finishing up, my phone dings with a text notification from Harmony stating she's almost at my house to pick me up. I long press on her message, giving her the thumbs up reaction as I find some shoes to throw on. A random thought to check in on Anthony pops up in my head. He's been so thoughtful to continuously check on me the past few months since Percy's death and if this were any other lifetime, I would even consider him my type. However, with my track record of constantly losing the people I love that are closest to me, that simply is not an option.

What would other people think anyways, if I were to show interest in someone else so soon?

My phone rings, bringing me out of my thoughts. It's Harmony letting me know she's outside. I toss my phone and keys into my purse as I grab it on the way out.

"Hey girl!" I say to Harmony as I enter her red Hyundai Sonata and close her car door.

"Now this is the Nelle I know! Look at you, looking all put together", she laughs as we pull out onto the road to head towards our favorite brunch spot.

"Hey, I know I should've asked first but you don't mind if Anthony joins us today, do you?"

I grimace with slight irritation before responding. "You *know* I don't like surprises but it's fine *this time*...I actually was just thinking about him right before you pulled up."

"I mean I keep saying y'all would make a cute couple!" She blurts out half-seriously, half-jokingly.

"I know but you know how I feel about that. One, it's so soon after Percy's death and two, he'll end up dying if I get too close to him."

"Chile boo, if that was the case I'd be dead!" retorts Harmony as she rolls her eyes then returns them to the road.

I laugh, "Yeah, you are quite the exception."

"You know once I bond to someone, I bond forever! Imma ride or die! Ain't no going back! But back to Anthony...let's just say hypothetically, if he were to ask you out for just a casual date, would you say yes?" Harmony asks me with a shimmer of mischievousness to her smile as we arrive at the restaurant.

I roll my eyes without answering as I exit her car. We enter the building and are greeted by a young hostess that takes us to our seats. Anthony has already arrived and greets us as soon as he spots us. He stands to pull out mine and Harmony's chairs.

He's such a gentleman.

"Hey ladies, how are y'all doing today?" He asks. "I didn't know what to get you to drink so I asked for 3 waters."

"Oh we're great now that there's food! I don't know 'bout y'all but I'm starving!" exclaims Harmony.

I laugh, "Girl, you always hungry! This ain't nothing new! I'm doing a lot better today, Anthony. Thank you for asking, how are you?"

"I'm great now that you're here", he replies with a wink.

Harmony swallows a sip of her water, "You know, you never did answer my question I asked as we arrived, Nelle. So yes or no to the date?"

"What a way to put me on the spot." I glare towards her. "But my answer is yes, just not right now. I have to get on with my life eventually, but I'm not ready right now."

Harmony squeals in delight, "That's my que, I'll see you fine folks in just a bit. I've got some business to take care of but I'll be inside if either one of you needs me."

And with that Harmony stands to grab her things and leaves Anthony and I to ourselves.

When I said yes to the date, I didn't mean right now. I don't know what I'm gonna do with that girl, I love her but she's gonna drive me to insanity.

"I take it Harmony kind of sprung this last minute outing on you...", Anthony smiles with humor in his eyes.

I chuckle, "It's not that it was last minute because she asked me a couple days ago if we could do brunch." I pause as I swallow a gulp of water, "but she didn't tell me you would be here until we were on the way. I also didn't know that it'd just be us two, although that part, I don't mind."

"I wasn't aware of that either but Harmony claims to know what she's doing", he laughs.

"I'm glad you're here though, I was just thinking of catching up with you right before she picked me up today."

"Is that right?" He half smirks. "And what kind of catching up are you talking?"

Completely missing his attempt at flirting I respond with a small giggle before answering. "Well, you've been a big part of my healing process and honestly I just wanted to thank you for putting up with me through all the ups and downs of the past few months."

"Janelle, you know it's nothing. I'm here for you always, you know that. I just don't want you to ever feel like you have to go through things alone," he says as he reaches for my hand. "That's the worst feeling I've ever endured and I wouldn't want my worst enemy to feel that way," his voice cracks just a bit with his last sentence.

"I know but it takes a strong man to listen to a woman cry about another man for hours at a time" I laugh out loud at the irony.

"Well, that's because I really care about you Janelle. I would love to actually take you out on a real date" he says nonchalantly as he glances around.

I reposition myself in my seat, pulling my hand back to run it through my locs. "One day...I'll be ready to date again with time."

He stiffens and purses his lips together at my statement. "It's been nearly five months, Nelle and we've spent most of that time together, getting to know each other." He lets out a slow breath before continuing, "I understand you're still grieving so I won't hold anything against you but I want it to be known that I would love the chance to sweep you off your feet."

I smirk as I take a sip of my virgin mimosa that was brought out during our conversation. "What makes you so sure you can sweep me off my feet?" I question flirtatiously as I flutter my eyelashes at him.

Anthony lets out a deep laugh, "I've grown to know you quite a bit, you prefer the simple things in life since your profession causes you a great deal of stress. Would you be opposed to a simple midday movie and lunch? That way it's not as official as a real date. We can go as friends."

"Let me think about it, okay? This isn't a yes but it isn't a no." I reply as I gaze into his dark brown eyes. They seem to lose the little sparkle of hope that was twinkling in them. He exhales in a slight huff but nods his head in agreement.

Harmony walks back out to join us just as our waitress arrives to take our order. I order the meat lover's omelette with extra cheese since this was one of mine and Percy's favorite things to eat during brunch.

"So, how are you two lovebirds?" Harmony questions as she hands her menu to the waitress.

I ignore her question as I finish off my fake mimosa. I'm lowkey annoyed with Harmony at how she sprung this whole brunch with Anthony on me. I despise being put in awkward situations.

Anthony answers "I wasn't very successful apparently."

"What? Are you serious?", she questions as she eyes me.

I shrug, "Harmony, you know how I feel about things being sprung up on me. I really would've appreciated more of a head's up", I turn to Anthony with a sincere grin on my face. "It wasn't a no, it was a 'not yet.'"

Anthony perks up "Hey, I'll take whatever I can get from you", and with that he stands to excuse himself to the restroom.

"Nelle, you know I didn't mean to upset you in any kind of way, I just want to see you happy again and the closest I've seen is when you're with Anthony." Harmony explains once we're alone.

"I know but it's just that I'm still mourning the loss of my husband and the loss of the family I once envisioned for my child. Trust me, it's not that I don't ever want to be happy again but at this time in my life I feel like it's wrong of me to be happy when the death of my husband is still so recent. I've never opened up to anyone the way I opened up to him and it hurts to know he may have possibly been cheating on me. I mean we *still* don't know who that mystery woman was that dipped at the scene. I feel like I have so many unanswered questions about his death."

"I get that, I truly do but as your best friend, I miss the person you used to be before all this happened. Yeah, you've always been afraid to get close to others due to your irrational fear of losing them but you're about to have a baby, Nelle", she exclaims as if it's the worst thing in the world to be pregnant and alone. "And Anthony is such a great guy. I mean after that whole ordeal my cousin's ghetto ass homegirl, he deserves someone that is actually gonna appreciate him."

I glance at her with a puzzled expression on my face, "What do you mean the ordeal with your cousin's homegirl? What happened?"

"Whew chile, where do I start? So remember the girl, La'Kyra, that stole Yasmin's boyfriend a few years back? Well, this hoe started dating Anthony in 2021 but took that man for granted. Honestly, she didn't know what to do with a man that treated her like a queen so she ended up fucking his friend Cameron and getting pregnant while her and Ant were still together. She let this man think he was the daddy of that ugly ass baby while knowing it wasn't his."

I shot Harmony a look because kids are usually off limits but instead she continued "and before you say anything...yeah I said it, all that girl's kids ugly. Ugly ass baby from a ugly ass mama! Fuck her and them kids!" she spits out. "There's barely any good black men left out here and that bitch wanna ruin this one because she doesn't know a good man when she sees one."

I'm taken aback because I never knew this about Anthony. Something about him seems just a bit too good to be true but apparently, he's had his fair share of heartbreak himself. I hit Harmony's leg to stop her from saying anything else about the situation as I glance behind her and notice Anthony walking back to our table.

As he sits, he notices the energy of the table is off. "Do I even want to know what was said while I was away?" he asks with a slight hint of humor in an attempt to soften the mood.

Harmony answers first, "Nah, no need...it was regarding a no good mammy of a woman."

"Ha...I know all too well about those.", he replies quietly with a hint of sadness about him.

16

Finally, I spot our young waitress as she glides towards us with our plates. I can't help but notice she favors me...a lot! She has the same mahogany brown eyes and round, high cheeked face as I do. She even has a dimple on her right cheek when she smiles just like I do. *Why do I feel as if I know her?*

She sets our plates down with grace as I check out her name tag...*Brandi*. I make a mental note to remember.

"Here ya go", says Brandi, "Would you like another virgin mimosa?", she asks as she eyes my glass.

"Yes, I'd love another," I reply.

"Would anyone else like another while I'm at it?"

"Yeah, I'll take another," Harmony responds.

"Me too," quickly adds Anthony reluctantly peeling his eyes away from Brandi.

"Alrighty then, I'll be right back with two real mimosas and one fake one!", Brandi says with a bright smile as she turns to leave our table.

Before I can even distract myself away from Brandi's similarities to me, Anthony speaks up.

"Damn, Nelle! She looks like she could be your long lost sister! You two look *JUST* alike!"

"Okay, cool...so I wasn't the only one who noticed that?" Harmony

17

questions.

"I literally was sitting here saying the same thing! Did my parents have another child and not tell me!?" I laugh while taking a delicious bite of my omelette.

"Remember that woman you saw at the funeral? Could it be her? You did say she resembled you from what you could tell", asks Harmony.

"Hmm...I actually didn't think about that but I don't think so. The woman I saw appeared to be older than our waitress." I pause, closing my eyes before continuing, "I hate not knowing who she is. I should've said something to her at the funeral." I mumble, taking a breath, "Now I'll never know. Sometimes I wish I could contact Percy for just one more conversation to get some answers."

"Well, they have these things called séances, you know", Harmony snickers.

"Séances!? That's some white people shit!" Anthony injects a little too loudly as we laugh. He peeks around us before lowering his voice, "You know us black folks don't fool around with spirits."

"No need to worry, I've never believed in that stuff anyway," I manage to get out after a fit of laughter. "Hell, for all I know, there could be no God. I mean what type of God would repeatedly take my loved ones away from me?"

Harmony interjects, "I mean, I'm just throwing it out there. My coworker knows this older African woman. I think she said her name is.... Hell, I can't remember but if you ever change your mind, let me know. But girl, don't start that mess. You're just going through a tough time right now, God's got you and I do too." She elbows me on the arm as rolls her eyes playfully.

Brandi walks over to our table with our glasses.

"I'm sorry, I don't mean to butt in but did I hear you say séance?"

I looked curiously at her, "Yeah, we were just kidding. We don't fool around with the dead."

"Good! I know of someone that started dibbling and dabbling with spirits. She made contact with some kind of entity and has never been the same."

"Well, I'm good on that", I exclaim "I've seen enough horror movies to know we should leave the dead where they are."

We all laugh but Harmony can't seem to help herself, "Are you from around here Brandi? You look like you could be related to Janelle," she says as she nods her head over at me.

"Oh, do I?" Brandi smiles and spins in a twirl as she glances over at me. "If I look like you then I'm doing great! You are gorgeous!"

I blush and wave her compliment off with a flip of my hand, "Don't make my head any bigger than it already is now!" I laugh, "but thank you."

"Nah, I'm not from around here. I grew up about three hours away from here in Bridgeport. I don't have any relatives here in Fairfield that I know of."

"You could literally pass for Janelle's younger sister," inserts Anthony with curiosity in his eyes, "What's your last name if you don't mind me asking?"

"It's Reynolds but I'm an only child, as is my mother," she quickly explains before glancing inside towards the kitchen. "I've got to get back to work but thank you much for the compliment, y'all! Let me know if you need anything else, mmkay?"

And with that she returns to waiting tables while we continue eating.

Chapter 3

Janelle

It's been over a week but I can't seem to get Brandi off of my mind. I'm tempted to call up Anthony, Harmony or even Raquel just to have a reason to go back to the restaurant in hopes of running into her again. I would love to know more about her background, maybe there is some kind of relation a few generations back in our lineage.

Almost as if he can read my thoughts, my phone rings, it's Anthony.

"Hey Anthony! Can you get out my head?" I say with amusement, "I was just thinking of calling you."

"Ha! Good luck with that, I'm tryna be the *only thing* on your mind. I was actually calling to see if you were ready to take me up on my offer."

"Hmm..." I say out loud while weighing my options. I think I like Anthony but I don't want to lead him on either. I want to be sure he knows this is a date just as friends.

"Sure, under one condition," I say cautiously while trying to interpret his facial expression.

He leans forward, anxiously "And that is?"
"I will agree to a date as friends. I don't want things to get weird between us" I answer.

He sits back, relief washing over his face. "Is that not what we are?" He questions with a smirk. "Of course I'm fine with that."

Okay, great! Just tell me the time and place..." I trail off for a second then continue, "actually, I was kinda hoping we could go back to where Brandi works. I want to learn more about her and also about what happened to the person she knows that started messing with spirits."

I can hear Anthony let out an exasperated exhale before saying "You're not thinking about having a séance, are you?" He halfheartedly jokes.

"What?! Oh no, no. Not at all!" I exclaim a bit taken back, "I'm just curious about what happened to this person and I would like to find out a little more about her."

"Oh, I see! You're using me as an excuse to get closer to a *woman* instead of me!" Anthony says sarcastically.

"Come on, Ant", I giggle and roll my eyes even though he's unable to see me. "You know it's not like that. I'm not sure how to describe it but I feel like I've met her before. Maybe I've seen her before, somewhere out shopping."

"I know, Nelle. I'm just fucking with you. You probably feel like you've seen her before because you two look alike." He lifts an eyebrow like The Rock then continues, "But serious question, are you not scared of séances and spirits and shit? My mama always said to never go looking for trouble because once you look, it'll surely find you."

I roll my eyes at that last sentence. Almost every Black person's mama or grandma has had a strange encounter with the spirit world. They then vow to never open that door again although it never truly closes because they still oblige by Hoodoo superstitions like not washing clothes or letting a man be the first person to enter your home on the first day of the year.

"I'm not looking for trouble, I'm looking for answers about my husband's death and whoever this woman is, that was in his vehicle." I snap sharply. "I deserve to know the truth, no matter how bad it may hurt."

I cycle through a plethora of emotions as I clench my fists in frustration at the situation. I begin bargaining with myself to prevent an outburst of emotions that I've been holding in. *There has to be a solid reason for Percy and this woman being together the night of his accident.*

"Look, I didn't mean anything by it except to just be careful." He clears his throat nervously before continuing, "I'd actually like to discuss something with you about Percy in person", says Anthony, "which is why I was calling to ask you out."

"Oh…I'm sorry, I kinda took the conversation left, huh?" I chuckle to lessen the tension.

"Yeah, but it's cool. I know you've been through a lot. How is everything with the baby? When's the next appointment?"

"The baby is fine, still feeling like a parasite draining my energy but I think the morning sickness is *finally* easing up a little more day by day. My next appointment is two weeks from now", I explain. "I'm only six and a half months so the appointments are still only once a month for now."

"Cool, cool. Well, you already know I'm here if you need me", replies Anthony. "So about this lunch date..."

"How about Friday at 11?" I answer with a question.

"It sounds like a date!"

"It's a date, I'll see you then", I pause, "Hey, Ant... Thank you for being patient with me."

"It's nothing." I hear him smile through his reply, "See you soon."

* * *

The Next Day

I hear my doorbell ring just as I finish slipping on some clothes. I run to let Harmony in, she's here to help me pick out something cute to wear on my lunch date. As I open the door, she rushes under the porch to avoid the downfall of rain.

"Girl, it took you long enough! I'm damn near drenched!" exclaims Harmony.

"It's barely a drizzle," I smart mouth her. "Just shut up and get your ass in here."

She steps in and sets her umbrella next to the door. I grab some sweet tea for the both of us from the kitchen in our favorite 'Golden Girls' cups and meet her in the living room. We take a sip as we find a seat on my fairly worn brown couch.

"So, Ant said he wants to talk to me about something in person." I say as I lower the cup from my lips. "I'm curious to know what it is, has he mentioned anything to you?"

Harmony gives me that 'bitch please' look.

"I know you ain't sitting here questioning me of all people! You know I can't hold water especially if it's concerning my good sis."

"I'm just making sure, chile," I laugh. "He made sure I didn't reach wanna out to anyone about the spirit world. He quoted his grandma and everything."

"Honestly, I don't see what the big deal is", says Harmony. "White people reach out to the dead through psychics all the time but when we do it, we're doing Black Magic. Gotta love good ole America and its double standards."

"Okay, Dr. Umar. Bring it back in", I laugh as I reel my imaginary fish reel back in.

I'm not in the mood for Harmony to go all hotep-ish on me right now about double standards and injustices on our people.

"I really hope Brandi is working. Doesn't she seem eerily familiar to you?" I question, hoping I'm not coming off as creepy.

"Nah, Nelle. She does look familiar but I'm pretty sure I'd recall if we had run into her before."

"Well, maybe we can ask her more about her family just to see if there's some kind of connection there."

"That's starting to sound kind of stalkerish. We should be more focused on this woman at the crash site and funeral. If you really want to try to find out more about her, you could always start with Percy's phone and bank records. I would've mentioned it sooner but you're just now getting used to your new normal." Harmony says emphatically. "You know, start with the easiest thing first."

"Or... We could start with the spirit world." I reply with a smirk.

"Oh! So you really tryna act like them white folks, huh?" she fires back as she tosses a burnt orange throw pillow my way.

We both lose it with laughter. We finish our tea and continue planning our detective work. I decide that Harmony's right, I should start with something as simple as phone records first.

"Imma go grab Percy's cell phone real quick. I haven't been able to turn it on because it's too painful to think of him no longer being here." I announce as I stand to exit the living room.

Once I reach our bedroom, I walk over to the night stand on what used to be Percy's side of the bed and open the top drawer where his iPhone sits fully charged but turned off. I grab the phone and run back to rejoin Harmony in the living room.

"Here it is", I say with hesitation as I turn the phone on. "I'll go through his messages first."

Harmony grabs my hands to prevent me from entering Percy's passcode into the phone.

"Nelle, wait," she says, "Are you prepared for whatever we may see in this phone?"

I exhale slowly and mutter, "I'm as ready as I'll ever be."

* * *

Ros: When are you going to introduce me to your wife?

Percy: I'm not. Didn't I tell you to never contact me again?

Ros: I'll do that after I've met Janelle.

Percy: She will never know about you. Contact me again and I'll make your life a living hell. Oh, and keep my wife's name out of your fucking mouth.

* * *

An hour and a half later, I'm still in the living room with Harmony and a face full of tears. Anthony has since joined us as I was too upset from my findings in Percy's texts to make our lunch date.

Harmony speaks first, "I'm so sorry Nelle, but at least you know the truth about the man you thought you knew."

Devastation isn't even the word. I don't recognize the immense emotions that I'm feeling right now. Pure misery, maybe? Whatever the word is, multiply that by ten.

"The truth doesn't make me feel any better!" I shout, "How could Percy be involved with another woman?! I thought he loved me."

"Sometimes those that lie to you only do so to protect your feelings." pipes up Anthony.

"But my husband tho, Ant!? How could he? I tried so hard to keep him happy and satisfied but apparently, my best still wasn't enough," I cry out in despair.

"Trust me, I'm not saying lying to you is okay, just that I understand him lying in order to spare your feelings. No one likes to hurt the people they love although lying can oftentimes hurt worse than the offense" explains Anthony. "Maybe it's a man thing."

"Are you fucking kidding me, saying that Percy hid an affair because he was trying not to hurt Nelle's feelings?", exclaims Harmony incredulously.

"Now, you're switching up my words." says Anthony exasperatedly,

"What I said was...."

"Just drop it!" I interject loudly. "I need to find out more about this 'Ros' person my husband was been talking to."

Chapter 4

Janelle

"Okay, so we have at least a start" says Anthony, while sitting back against my brown couch and rubbing his hands together like Birdman.

"Yeah, you handle the reverse phone number look up while at work and we'll go from there," I reply. "Maybe I could hire a private investigator if we can find out Ros' full name."

Harmony jerks her head towards me, "Aht, aht! No ma'am, I got a homegirl whose detective skills are top notch. I promise with only a name she can find anything, or in this case anyone."

"Does she have her own office I can visit for a consultation?" I ask, truly intrigued.

"Girl, nah! I just know her from Facebook. She's an internet detective but don't let that fool you! She has helped a few police departments around this area with missing persons cases. She's the real deal."

"Let me think about it, I really don't want anyone else knowing my business." I sigh, before teasing, "Yo ass probably threw that police department line in there to sound good."

"You know me so well," smirks Harmony.

"You get on my damn nerves, if I didn't love you so much, I'd hate you!" I sarcastically chuckle with her.

Anthony stands, grabbing his jacket and keys on his way up.

"Well, I better get going ladies. I gotta work tomorrow," he states as Harmony and I simultaneously stand to walk him out.

"Yeah, I better get going too, Janelle. Anthony let us know if anything turns up when you look up that phone number", says Harmony.

"Fa sho. You know I got y'all. I'll do anything I can to help, and Janelle," he pauses to look at me with that irresistible crooked half smile he does sometimes, "I'd still love that lunch date."

"How about the same time tomorrow at The Chew. Hopefully Brandi will be there." I answer.

"You've almost burnt me out on Mexican food Nelle, but whatever you want, I'm down", he replies. "I'll pick you up at ten-thirty tomorrow morning?"

"Sure thing but you do realize they sell more than just Mexican food, right?" I question him teasingly. "I really wanna thank you both. I know I'm such a mess and this pregnancy isn't helping. I feel like my emotions are all over the place."

"Chile, we know you're a hormonal mess right now. Just be glad we love you because I damn sure wouldn't be putting up with this mess for anyone else." Harmony smiles and adds quickly.

"Yeah, Nelle. You're family to us, you don't have to thank us for anything. Real families like us stick together through the ups and downs." agrees Anthony.

I'm such a crybaby (or maybe it's the baby) that I burst out in tears and grab each of them for a group hug.

With tears streaming down my face I blurt out, "I love you two so much! I would have never survived these past few months without the two of you."

"Alright now, that's enough girl. I didn't get you calmed down just to cry happy tears as we leave." Harmony insists, trying her best to hide her forming tears.

"I know, I'm sorry!" I sniffle, "It's just that you know my family dynamics. I've always felt so alone in this world and I want to make sure you two know how grateful I am to have you in my life. I don't take either one of you for granted because I know firsthand how quickly life can change."

We all hug one last time then Anthony dashes out the front door at full speed in attempt to avoid the steady downfall of rain.

Harmony grabs her still wet umbrella as she exits the door.

"Y'all, drive safe in this weather", I yell out "and text me when you're home!"

* * *

The next morning, I grab my purse and phone as I head out the door to meet Anthony.   He arrives at exactly 10:30 to pick me up and surprisingly, I'm not running behind.

I open the door to greet him, "Hey Ant, you look... amazing but you smell delicious!" I say as I look him up and down while inhaling his unique scent.

Anthony is dressed in some well fitted black jeans with a plain white tee and a gray distressed jean jacket. The white t-shirt hugs his masculine frame making him look simply irresistible.

That combined with his low top faded haircut has me wanting to wrap myself around him. I guess pregnancy really does bring out the sexual nature in women.

He smiles as he eyes me up and down. Luckily, it's a bright, sunny day with a temperature of 76 degrees and not very much humidity so I decided on a black and white sundress with red, yellow and blue color block patterns.

"Not as amazing as you", he replies still smiling. "So, you ready to go?"

"I got ready a little early so I've been ready" I admit, slightly embarrassed by that revelation. "Let's go!"

Anthony being the gentleman that he is, walks me to his white GMC Sierra and opens the door for me. *I could get used to this,* I think to myself.

Anthony closes my door after I've seated and walks around to the driver's side to hop in. I must admit, I do miss Percy like crazy but it is nice to have a man look out for me the way Ant has.

Suddenly I feel a weird sensation in my belly. I'm not sure if it's gas or…could it be the baby!?

It's such an indescribable feeling, almost like a butterfly fluttering inside. Is this what the first movements of a baby feel like? I guess I could ask Ant but 1. He's a guy so he'll never know and 2. He doesn't have any kids either.

"Is everything alright Nelle?" Anthony says while glancing over at me, "You look uncertain about something. If you've changed your mind about the lunch date, that's fine. I'm not upset or anything."

He snaps me out of my thoughts. "No, it's fine. I want to go on this date. I just don't know if what I felt was the baby moving or not. It was sort of like a feeling of bubbles popping", I reply.

Anthony's face lights up, "Yeah, five and a half months with your first. That sounds about right for movement" he says.

I laugh out loud. "And just how would you know that as a man?"

"I may not have any kids of my own but I've been around women that were pregnant before. I've heard all the good, bad and straight up ugly that comes with pregnancy. My sister lived at home during most of her pregnancy so I know how aggravating y'all can get."

My eyes perk up because in the short time I've known Anthony, he's never once mentioned anything about his family. I wasn't even aware he had a sister.

"I didn't know you had a sister! Does she live out of town or something?" I ask before I notice a hit of pain in his eyes.

"Well, she passed away some years back suddenly so it's hard to bring her up without me getting in my feelings", he replies.

I immediately feel terrible for asking. "I'm so sorry, I didn't know or else I wouldn't have asked that."

"My family life wasn't the best and after my sister passed away it completely fell apart." Anthony explains. "I'm not sure what happened but my mom and my sister had this huge falling out over something right before she died. All I can remember is my mom saying that over and over."

"Wow, I'm sorry to hear that. I guess that's what makes all families unique. We're all dysfunctional in some way or another." I answer.

"But back to you," he says, shaking the painful thoughts away. "I've been told a baby's first movements feels like fish swimming around inside your womb."

"Well, let's hope that's what it was because otherwise I may be a bit gassy," I reply before bursting into a fit of laughter.

"Just make sure you let down that window before letting it loose!" Anthony jokes while gravitating his eyes towards the window button on my side of the vehicle.

Within minutes, we are pulling up at my favorite spot, The Chew. Anthony exits the truck and jogs over to my door, opening it and helps me out. We head towards the entrance and are greeted by a young, blonde hostess. She seats us outside and gets Brandi as our server at my request. After about five minutes, Brandi heads over to greet us.

"Hey y'all! Back again so soon, huh?", she greets us with a smile that could brighten the darkest room. "What can I get ya?"

I grin and reply, "Hi Brandi, how are you today?"

"I'm great! It's my Friday, I *need* these next couple of days off."

"I bet, I can recall in my younger years when I worked as a server for two weeks before quitting. That was some of *thee* hardest work I've ever done. My feet were barking!" I explain and continue, "I was actually hoping to catch you again to learn a little more about the person that held the séance."

Brandi looks surprisingly confused for a second before her smile returns to her face, showing the deep dimple in her cheek that's identical to mine.

"Oh..! That's not where I thought this conversation was going," she laughs "but sure I can. I don't really know much about the woman because I only met her a few times when I was younger but after making contact with the spirit world, she was….different. My mom wouldn't allow me around her after that."

"Well, if you have time today I would love to hear all about it. Spooky things have always fascinated me." I reply as Anthony slightly displays an irritated facial expression that's barely noticeable.

"I got you, I get off in just a bit so I can explain it all then if y'all are still here." She says, looking between me and Anthony, "Until then, what can I get you two?"

"Ladies first", says Anthony, nodding his head towards me from across the table.

"Oh, I'll have the chicken and cheese quesadilla with the rice and beans. I'd also like an order of queso dip with a sweet tea to drink." I quickly order, partly because I'm starving and partly because I always order the same thing at this restaurant unless this baby is making me crave an omelette like last time I was here.

"And I'll have the chicken fajitas with corn tortillas, extra guacamole and a Sprite to drink." Anthony adds.

Brandi does a little bounce after she writes down our order and slides the notepad into her apron pocket. "Alright, I've got it! I'll be back in a sec with your drinks." Then she turns and walks back inside.

"So", I turned back towards Anthony "what was it you wanted to talk to me about?"

"Damn, you can't even let the conversation flow into that direction?" He says. "But that's what I like about you, you're very direct and straight to the point." He stiffens just a bit as he clears his throat and adjusts himself in his seat. "It's about Percy, are you okay with me speaking about him?" He replies with a stone expression on his face that I can't seem to read.

"Uh, yeah. That's...That's fine," I stammer with concern. Now I'm full of worry due to the unreadable expression plastered on Anthony's face.

"Okay, good. So... I wanted to bring this up before now but I wasn't sure where your head was at," he ushers out quickly. "You're probably not gonna like what I say."

I've already told him it's okay, I'm not one for beating around the bush. Also, this pregnancy isn't helping with the minuscule amount of impatience I have.

"Would you just spit it out, Ant?" I hiss toward him, irritably.

Just as he's about to reply, Brandi strolls back over with our drinks.

"One Sprite for you and one sweet tea and queso for you", she says cheerily while carefully setting our glasses and the small bowl of queso down.

I glance at her as I readjust my tone and attempt to hide my irritation. "Thank you Brandi."

"No problem, do you need anything else?"

"No, I think we're all set for now" says Anthony.

"K, just holla at me if you need anything."

Anthony turns back to me as Brandi walks off. "Alright, back to what I was saying... Percy was seen multiple times in what appeared to be inappropriate interactions with one inmate in particular," he spits out, taking a deep breath, clearly relieved to have gotten that off his chest.

"I didn't think anything of it until I ran into him at the corner store one night... with her. She was recently released on parole but they spent quite a bit of time together in the short time I worked there while she was an inmate."

I feel myself catch a breath. It takes a minute to fully process what Anthony is saying. *They spent a lot of time together.* No, I don't think *he's saying what I think he's saying.* I go through a plethora of emotions within seconds.

"Anthony..." I stop him, seriousness settling in my tone.

He continues, "I think he may have been seeing her, romantically."

I cut him off again, "Anthony." I fume, displaying the coldness in my voice. "Be. Fucking. For. Real. Why would you just now bring this up? You've let me worry all this fucking time about who this woman was at my husband's funeral yet you've known all along who she is?" I angrily exclaim.

"It's not like that. Like I said I saw them a handful of times when I first started at FCI Fairfield but a week later she made parole. I didn't think anything of it because it was damn near two months later that I saw them together down at Bunyan's corner store," he immediately explains. "Then it was another two months before Percy's death. His death came as such a shock to everyone at work, that seeing him and her together was the last thing on my mind. I knew I recognized the name Ros, I just couldn't recall where I had seen it until I looked up that number."

"The reverse number look up pulled up the inmate's name?" I ask somberly.

"Yeah, I figured it'd be best to start the search on computer applications at work that I can easily access first. I entered the number into our database since we keep recently released inmate's information in house and it led me to Inmate #16009. Rosetta Hamilton."

Finally, I have a name. But why would Percy risk our marriage for an *inmate*? This has to be wrong. I take a deep breath, exhaling slowing through my nose and counting to five before I respond.

"I really appreciate this information, Ant but there has to be some type of misunderstanding," I reason as I shake my head in disagreement. "There's no way in hell Percy would risk losing everything we've worked so hard together for."

He reaches across the table for my hand but I pull back. "Janelle, I'm sorry to bring you this type of news but that's what it's looking like. I can do a little further investigation of my own or ask my buddy to do some digging" he suggests.

I feel a slow burning rage rising in me. I can't believe the nerve of this man to actually suggest my husband cheated on me and with *an inmate*!?

40

I knew something was off about him to me. He's probably just saying this in hopes of me falling for him. *Well I'm not buying it.*

"Just let me know how I can help", he continues.

"How you can help?" I huff, "You can help by *not* helping! If your first thought after seeing the two of them together is an affair then I don't need your help. It's clear you didn't know Percy very well at all."

He looks taken aback, "Nelle, I was only trying to help. I didn't mean to offend you in any way, I was just stating the most likely possibility."

"That's not the most likely possibility! He was the Warden after all. He built personal relationships with most of the inmates in one way or another. He was a good man! A damn good one and I'll be damned if you try to paint him in this negative light."

"Look, I apologize—" he says, throwing his hands up like he's under arrest but I cut him off.

"Just drop it, Ant. I'm done with this conversation." I spit out, "I'm going to the restroom."

I stand to excuse myself from the table. Tears are lining my eyes, threatening to escape, as I enter the building and direct myself to the bathroom.

Just as I open the door I nearly collide into Brandi, who is exiting the bathroom.

"Whoa, my bad!" she exclaims just before glancing upward and noticing it's me she's nearly run into. "Hey, are you okay?"

I wipe the one tear that has rolled down my cheek as I steady myself again. "Oh gawd! I'm such a mess. It's the pregnancy." I shamefully joke in an attempt to make light of the situation.

"Oh Hun, come here." She says as she pulls me into the bathroom. "What's going on? Are you in pain? Your friend isn't being an asshole, is he?"

She pulls me into a warm embrace. It is unexpected but seems to be exactly what I need at that moment. As I straighten up I catch a glimpse of myself in the mirror. *Great, now everyone can tell I'm upset.* I pull a few locs back with a finger and wipe underneath my eyes with a paper towel.

"I'm fine, I just found out some devastating news about my late husband. He may have been cheating on me." I sputter out that last sentence with disdain.

"I'm so sorry. I can't imagine how you're feeling." Brandi replies quietly as she rubs a hand along my shoulder.

I stammer, "No... No, I'm the one that should be sorry. This is my dilemma, it isn't yours. He's gone, I know but it still hurts to think the worst of him."

"I understand," she responds. "I'm not really sure if it would help but we can talk about it, if you'd like. I'm a non-judgmental ear."

"I'm okay, it just hurts hearing this from *him*," I answer as I glance towards the door. "I don't know whether he's telling me this because he thinks it'll make me forget about my husband and fall for him or if he's being sincere. I mean I do enjoy my time with him but with him accusing my husband of being a cheater, it makes me question his motive. He did seem to pop up out of nowhere after Percy's death." I shake away those thoughts to attempt to regain my composure.

"Everything will all work out. If it's in the past, leave it in the past", she says and then gives a small chuckle. "I feel like this is the wrong time to say this but I don't think I caught your name."

I let out a soft laugh at the randomness of her statement as I realize I never gave her my name. "I'm sorry. My name is Janelle."

"Janelle, got it." She smiles. "Well, if you are okay then I'm gonna go grab your plates to bring to your table before clocking out."

"Actually, before you go could you tell me a little about that séance?" I ask before she can leave.

"Sure, I don't know much though, only what I was told by my mom," she explains. "Wanna go grab a seat at the bar for a second?"

"Sure. Let's go", I reply.

Chapter 5

Janelle

I follow Brandi to the bar in the center of the restaurant. I settle in my seat as she turns towards me.

"So what would you like to know?" She asks.

"What exactly happened to the person that held the séance? How long ago was this?

Brandi thinks for a moment, "I'm not sure when this took place but my mom knew of a woman that gave birth to a set of twins, only one was a stillborn. Although she went on to have another baby, she never really recovered from that incident. So she decided to attempt to make spiritual contact with the child she lost."

I feel a tug at my heartstrings at the mention of a stillborn. That is a type of heartbreak I never wish to experience. If anything were to happen to my baby there'd be nothing else to live for.

"Evidently she made contact but it was with a malevolent spirit that caused her to lose her mind and kidnap a few kids over the course of a few years" she continues. "Last I heard of her, she was serving time in prison at FCI Fairfield."

My mouth drops, *could this be the same woman Percy was seen with?*

"Did this happen here in Fairfield? What was her name?" I question her.

"Nope, this was back at home in Bridgeport" she explains. "But I can't recall her name. I was a little girl when I saw her and was told to stay far away from her. That was the last time I remember ever seeing her. No one really talked about her because as kids there were rumors that whoever discussed her would summon the evil spirit that tricked her into kidnapping those kids."

"Gotta love small town rumors", I say. "Some of the most unique stories are started in them."

"Yeah, I was terrified of her when I was younger but as I got older I just stopped believing the séance had anything to do with losing her mind. She was just crazy from the get go according to people in town." She pauses, "Are you planning on having one?"

I shake my head in disagreement. "No, I've just always been curious about the spirit world, that's all. I'll leave talking to spirits to the white folks on those ghost hunting shows", I laugh.

Brandi smiles, "That's all I know about it and unfortunately, my mom won't talk about her." She stands from her seat, "I better go grab your plates or my manager may ask why I was late clocking out."

"Right, yeah." I reply before stopping her, "Hey, could you make it to go, please?"

"You got it. I'll meet y'all at your table with your food." She says before turning towards the kitchen.

* * *

I was so enthralled with the conversation with Brandi that I nearly forgot about Anthony. My annoyance quickly returns when I see him again. He looks worried, he knows he's fucked up by insinuating Percy would cheat on me.

"Oh, you're back!" He tries to joke lightly. "I thought you had gotten lost for a minute, I was about to come looking for you."

"I was fine, thanks." I say flatly, "I ran into Brandi while inside. I wanted to catch her before she got off work."

"So what'd you find out?" he inquires.
    "That the woman she knows of simply lost her mind after having a stillborn." Surprise lines his face as if he wants to say something but decides against it.

Luckily, I spot Brandi emerging from inside with two to-go boxes.

"Here y'all go! Is this two checks or one?" She asks while eyeing me.

"Split it please, Brandi." I answer her quickly.

"No, Janelle. I've got it, I asked you out." Anthony quips, pulling his wallet from his back pocket.

"Thanks but I'll take care of my own food."I reply before looking back at Brandi, awaiting the check.

"I brought it both ways just in case," says Brandi. "Here's yours and this one's yours." She says as she hands each one of us our check and turns to walk away.

We pay in an awkward silence and leave. I'm still upset with Anthony's accusations about Percy. I want nothing more than to separate myself from him.

The ride home was an uncomfortable one that didn't seem to end soon enough. After a 15 minute ride, we finally reached my house.

"Nelle, I want to apologize if I came off accusatory. I didn't mean to upset you." Anthony stammers swiftly before I have a chance to reach for the door handle.

I can see the truthfulness of his words in his eyes. *Maybe he does mean that.* I halfheartedly utter a "Thanks" his way as I close the truck door and head towards my front door.

Chapter 6

Janelle

The next day I'm still not in the mood to come to terms with what Anthony has told me. There is just no way Percy would do that to me. *I knew him better than anyone...or at least, that's what I thought.*

I'm missing Percy extremely badly today and I want nothing more than to hear his voice, touch his face, kiss his lips. Lord knows I would give anything to be able to see him one more time.

"I miss you P. I could really use a sign that this isn't true," I say out loud, "I don't know what to believe. I know for a fact you loved me so something tells me that Anthony is wrong about you."

I walk over to Percy's closet in our bedroom to pull out one of his nice dress shirts that still smells like him. I haven't touched his things since he left me. I've tried yet I can't bring myself to do it right now with all the extra hormones I'm experiencing due to being pregnant.

I lift the shirt and inhale, instantly I'm hit with his unique scent. It fills my nose and brings up the happy times that we shared together.

I can still envision his exact look plastered across his face as I hinted that we were pregnant. The surprise on his face was nearly suppressed by the pure happiness immediately displayed once he realized what I was saying.

One moment I'm smiling and reminiscing and the next I'm grief stricken all over again.

As sadness takes over, I decide to go to the living room to look through photos of our memories together.

I go past the couch over to a photo album located on the top shelf of the built in bookcase. I pull it down and open it to a picture of Percy and I when we were seniors. He was the star football player at our high school while I was the nerdy librarian's assistant.

He always made sure to include me in his activities. That included hanging out with his friends, all games and even parties, although I only ever attended one.

It's ironic how we were once good friends in high school that eventually went our different ways after graduation yet we ended up married. Harmony says we were destined from our first encounter. Honestly, if it weren't for her we probably never would have met.

Harmony was co-captain of the cheerleading squad and one of very few Blacks on the squad, similar to how Percy was nearly the same on the football team. Naturally, since they were the two 'star' Black kids, the entire school wanted them to get together but they quickly realized they argue worse than brother and sister.

That's when Harmony got the bright idea to play matchmaker which turned out great but ultimately we wanted different things. So we thought it would be best to just remain friends.

After graduation, we didn't see each other again until our 10 year class reunion. By that point Percy's muscles had filled out in all the right places and while I still had a thing for him, I was sure he didn't feel the same.

It wasn't until just before the reunion was over that he drunkenly approached me and confessed that he had never gotten over me. Truth be told, neither had I.

We literally picked up right where we left off. His dream of being a professional NFL player was cut short after he got injured during his first season with the Jacksonville Jaguars. And well... I was still a librarian, only I was now working at the local public library with hopes of one day opening my very own bookstore.

I pull out a photo of us on our wedding day. That was such a perfect day. Bright and sunny. Breezy weather. And my fine as hell husband.

I loved how small and intimate our wedding was. Only our closest family and friends were invited, all ten of them.

Memories of our wedding day encapsulates me with a warming sensation that radiates from my heart.

I smile, "Thanks for the best time of my life, P."

As I replace the photo then close and put away the album, I spot our wedding video. Just as I decide to turn it on, taking a seat on the couch still with Percy's shirt, my phone rings. It's Harmony.

"Hello?" I answer.

"Girl, what the hell happened yesterday? Anthony called me asking if I would talk to you for him."

"He's just doing too much." I reply matter of factly.

"And by that you mean..." questions Harmony.

"Long story short, he knew all along about an inmate that Percy was apparently seeing. I don't believe it though, I knew Percy. He wouldn't do that but Ant seemed set on that conclusion," I explain. "He *claims* he didn't recall seeing them together until he did the reverse number lookup."

"Which is probably true, Nelle," agrees Harmony.

"Okay..." I trail off.

Whose side is she on anyways?

"But I just wasn't in the head space to hear that. Maybe it's denial, maybe it's the pregnancy but I can't make myself believe any of that right now. It will literally break me."

"And I understand that Nelle but you can't get upset and drop people when they say something you don't agree with. I honestly think he had good intentions when he told you this, he wouldn't want to hurt you purposely." She points out, "He's only trying to help you just like you asked."

This is not the conversation I wanted to have with Harmony. She's making complete sense and I know it.

I sigh, "Yeah, I know. I was probably a bit too harsh on him but I can't think of Percy in that way, as a cheater. I'm barely holding it together as it is."

There's a moment of hesitation before Harmony responds.

"Janelle, the love you two shared was real. Whether he cheated or not ain't what's important. What matters is figuring out why she was with Percy if he wasn't cheating. If you don't want to believe he was cheating, then don't but if you *really* want to know the truth about this woman then I'm gonna need you to be ready to accept the truth, no matter how difficult that may be."

As badly as I don't want to admit it, she's right. I did agree to their help in figuring out the truth behind this woman.

"I know, I know. It isn't Anthony I should be upset at, he's only helping. It's just that I have all these different emotions bottled up inside of me, I've never in my life been as emotional as I have been during this pregnancy."

"I think you should apologize to Anthony. He was really upset knowing he upset you.", states Harmony.

"Yeah, maybe I should call and invite him over but could you maybe come too just so things won't be so awkward?" I ask hopefully.

"Well, how about you text him to see if he's able to come by first and then let me know and I'll be right over."

"Why do you always have to make so much sense?" I laugh as I put my phone on speakerphone and open up my Messages app to text Anthony.

Hi Ant, I think we should talk. Are you able to come over? I type out.

I see the text bubbles appear and take that as a good sign. I immediately think to let him know that Harmony will be present also.

Harmony is coming, I'd really like it if you could join us too.

He must be thinking about it because the text bubbles have disappeared.

"Well, let's see what he says when he responds", I say to Harmony just as his reply pops up.

I'll be there in an hour.

"Okay, he'll be here in an hour. Can you be here by then?" I ask because I know Harmony is notorious for running on 'Black folks' time.

"Don't try me like that…I'll do you one better! I'll be there before Anthony." She says with a smirk in her response before she disconnects the call.

* * *

I decide to straighten up my place before they arrive by putting my dishes away, picking up any trash and folding the throw blankets that are tossed carelessly across my furniture. Once that's done, I spray my dreadlocks with water, add a little oil to spruce them back up and rub some moisturizer onto my face.

My doorbell rings just as I'm about to change into something more presentable than some old, holey black leggings and an over sized Beyonce t-shirt.

That's the fastest Harmony has EVER gotten dressed, I think to myself as I head towards the door.

To my surprise, I see Anthony standing at there with a blank expression on his face. I'm sure he's a bit uneasy due to our last encounter with each other.

"Hi Anthony," I say cheerfully as I invite him in. "I thought you were Harmony!"

"Hey Nelle, did I arrive too early?" He asks, looking back towards his truck.

"Nah, it's fine. This actually gives me time to apologize for my behavior yesterday. I shouldn't have snapped at you the way I did. I don't think I was prepared to hear what you said but if I want the truth, then I'm gonna have to woman up."

"Janelle, it's cool. I didn't even take your feelings into consideration. I realize now, that maybe I should have handled the conversation in a more sensible way to acknowledge and validate your feelings," he explains as we take a seat at my kitchen table.

"No, this isn't your fault. It's mine, I don't know what this pregnancy is doing to me but I'm all over the place," I reply. "Would you like anything to drink?"

"Yeah, lemme get a.... Hell, just give me whatever you're having," he answers.

I walk to the cabinet and retrieve two cups, fill them with ice and pour the two of us some sweet tea. I hand one cup to Anthony as I take a seat perpendicular to him.

He reaches out across the table for my hand and I swear my heart flutters and I forget to breathe for a second. Anthony leans inward closer to me, while rubbing his thumb across the back of my hand.

"Janelle..." He says in a deep, smooth voice while staring at me in the eyes.

It feels as if he's looking into my soul when he gazes at me this way. I feel myself melt, getting lost in his caramel-tinted, brown eyes.

"I like you... a lot," he says, pausing to study my face then continues. "I care about you, you're a part of my life again. And I don't want that to ever change."

I'm taken aback because I can't figure out what he means by 'a part of his life *again'* unless he thought we'd never speak again after yesterday. *Yeah, that's what it's gotta be,* I think to myself. I'm actually touched by the sentiment because as important as he is in my life, I didn't know whether I was just as important to him. I give his hand a small squeeze.

"I care about you too, Anthony and thank you. I promise I'm not going anywhere," I let out a slight chuckle. "It's nice to know how you feel about me...I think I feel the same."

"Is that right?" He questions with his eyebrows raised.

"From the very first time we met, I've felt this strange connection to you. It's almost like God, the Universe or whatever the hell is out there, has been telling me that you are meant to be in my life."

He slides his chair closer to me, "I feel it too, Nelle. The moment I first saw you, I was drawn to you."

"I probably shouldn't be saying this but maybe in another lifetime we could've met first," I damn near whisper.

Anthony gives a slight smirk, kisses my hand and says "It could be us during this one."

He slides his chair out as he stands while grabbing my other hand and pulling me to a stance with him. There is barely any space between us now. So close that I can almost taste his minty breath on my lips.

"Would it be wrong of me to fall for you while mourning my husband?" I mutter shamefully, nearly inaudible.

Before I can question anything else, Anthony tries to pull me into a tighter embrace, forgetting about my growing belly momentarily.

"Oh! Watch the baby!" I exclaim while rubbing my bump.

Anthony looks down with concern in his eyes, he reaches out to rub my stomach just as we both feel the baby move.

"Was that— was that the baby?!" He asks in shock.

I lift up my head so I'm looking at him and smile, "Yes, she just moved."

"I think I'm gonna take that as a good sign," he laughs. "Even your baby likes me! But I hope her mommy likes me too."

I feel my cheeks redden, due to the fact this is the most forward Anthony has ever been towards me. Unsure of how to respond, I blurt out "She does."

He glances at my mouth and back to my eyes again before coming closer to me. Less than two inches from me are his lips, so full and perfectly moisturized. I lift my face so that my lips are aligned with his as he slowly meets my mouth, our lips colliding.

His tongue presses against my lips, gently prying them open as he searches for my tongue. I pull back slightly, biting his bottom lip before fishing my tongue back into his mouth.

'Ding Dong.' "Someone is at your front door," states my Alexa Echo speaker, yanking us from the moment we just shared.

I take a step back, wiping the wetness from my lips as warmth radiates throughout my body.

"I, uh… I better get that." I manage to stumble out, grinning too hard like a schoolgirl with a crush.

I check myself out in the mirror centered along the hall before answering the door. The last thing I need is for Harmony to immediately start interrogating me. Unlocking the deadbolt, I hold the door open, standing back to allow Harmony inside.

"I ain't tryna hear it about being late, you know I gotta live up to our stereotype," she throws out with a wave of her hand, as she enters my home. "Where is Anthony? Everything good with y'all or should I figure out which one of you I should side with?

"I can't stand you," I say, rolling my eyes at her. "Anthony's in the kitchen."

"Cool, cool. So all is well. Have you apologized?" She asks just as Anthony joins us in the living room.

"She has and she's been forgiven," he answers with a short laugh.

Harmony crosses her arms, dramatically. "So, what the hell am I here for? I thought you needed me as a peacemaker, Nelle."

"Girl, shut up and sit down," I reply sarcastically to her as we all find a seat in the living room.

Chapter 7

Janelle

After hours of playing UNO and clowning each other, Anthony and Harmony eventually grow tired of me whooping their ass.

"I hate this game," says Harmony. "I'd rather play Spades or something. That way I can make it 'do what it do' regardless of what's in my hands."

I nod, "Yeah, I'd prefer Spades but we'd need one more person."

"Two more," Anthony interjects quietly almost as if he didn't want us to hear.

Harmony slams her cards down on the table in disbelief. "Nigga what!?"

I immediately reach across to Anthony with my hand out.

"Hand it here," I state matter of factly. "Right now."

"Daaaamn, y'all gon' do me like this?" Anthony laughs as he places an imaginary 'Black Card' in my palm.

We all burst into laughter. I've relaxed a bit since the intensity of earlier has partially diminished. *What was I thinking?* I shake my head slightly in disgust with myself.

"Earth to Janelle." I hear Harmony say off in the distance, reeling my thoughts back into the present.

"Huh?" I ask, "What was that?"

"Would you like to know what else Anthony found out? According to him, he couldn't finish because you stormed off."

I was so blindsided from Anthony's revelation that I didn't realize there was anymore to be said. *Am I okay to do this? Can I keep my cool no matter what's revealed?* I go back and forth a few times before coming to a conclusion.

"Yes." I take a moment to reconsider but decide against it. "Yeah. I would definitely like to know."

I glance over at Anthony with a reassuring smile. He dips his head in acknowledgment.

"Okay, well— ahem. Once I knew Ros's full name and recalled that she was recently released, I decided to contact Craig down at the courthouse to view her probationary terms. I have her contact number and address now. Per her Probation Agreement Ros is required to work. At the time this was printed," he says as he retrieves a yellow manila envelope "she hadn't found employment but this database is updated weekly so we should know pretty quickly once she finds employment."

He lifts up the two prongs and slides a finger under the folded flap pulling papers containing information about a woman inmate. *A woman inmate that may have been having an affair with my husband.* I swipe the papers from Anthony's grasp instantaneously.

ROSETTA D. HAMILTON
  INMATE ID: 16009
  PAROLE OFFICER : MARCUS JENKINS
  DOB: 10/31/1960
  ADDRESS: 9296 Gadsden St
  APT: K77
  HOWIE, SC 29001
  PHONE: 854-555-7313
  EMPLOYMENT: UNDETERMINED AT THIS TIME
  PERSONAL CONTACT(S):
  SHARON REYNOLDS
  ADDRESS REDACTED
  ADDRESS REDACTED
  PHONE: 854-555-9296
  DETAILS:
HAMILTON-16009 WAS RECENTLY TERMINATED FROM HER
POSITION AT WAFFLE KING
AS A SERVER DUE TO NOT
WORKING WELL WITH OTHERS. HAMILTON-16009 IN-FORMED ME OF INTERVIEW AS A HOUSE CLEANER WITH SHARON REYNOLDS' HOME CLEANING BUSINESS 'HELPING HANDS HOUSE CLEANING SERVICES.' WILL KNOW OUT-

COME BY THE END OF THE WEEK.
  M. JENKINS

I exhale slowly, releasing the breath I didn't know I was holding as I look back at the top left corner, where a photograph of Rosetta is stapled. *She definitely looks like she could be the woman from the funeral.*

After reading over the document, Anthony continues."So I was thinking maybe we could try calling her and asking a few questions first and if that leads us nowhere, maybe we could swing by her place or contact her personal contact, Sharon."

This is a lot to take in. The thought of her admitting to an affair with Percy is overwhelming to say the least. *I still have to believe in my heart that he wouldn't hurt me like that. Maybe it's all just a misunderstanding. She could be someone from Percy's childhood like a long lost aunt or something.*

Anthony casts cautious eyes toward me awaiting my response.

"This shit just got real, you guys," I say "but I'm ready for answers."

My stomach begins to knot at the thought of speaking with Rosetta Hamilton.

"Shall we try now?" questions Harmony as she sips her tea.

"I thought it might be best to call while we're present just so that you have all the support you may need. We can do it now or whenever you're ready" states Anthony delicately. "It's whatever you want."

They're both awaiting my reply but truth be told, I'm quite scared of the truth. If there was in fact an affair, will that change how I feel about this pregnancy? Will I still love this baby? A cheater's baby? *Maybe I could give her up for adoption*, the thought comes but goes as suddenly as it appeared.

"And he didn't tell you anything else?" I overhear Harmony asking Anthony.

Anthony side eyes me, shifting in his seat uncomfortably before answering. "No, he said he'd get back to me."

"Who is getting back to you?" I question, slightly puzzled.

"Oh, it's just Anthony's friend. You know, the private investigator. We're lucky, they go way back because he's doing all of this free of charge." Harmony blurts out faster than Anthony has time to stop her but she knows it's too late. "You didn't know about that... Did you?"

Anthony gives Harmony a death glare before turning to me. "Nelle, I was going to tell you but you got upset so quickly the other day that I didn't have time to mention I got some information from an old buddy of mine."

"And your buddy just so happens to be a private investigator?"

"Well, yeah," he says nervously, running one hand over his head. "He is but technically this doesn't count as any 'work' for him, just a favor for an old friend.

"But you deliberately went against what I specifically asked you **not** to do." I spit out in disgust.

I feel my heart rate quicken as my blood begins to boil. There's an itching in my body to take all my frustrations out on him but I try my best to reframe.

As if he can sense my extreme desire to smack the shit out of him right now, he scoots to the far end of my couch.

"I don't need any more of your help, Anthony." I hiss with a coldness that freezes the room.

"Come on, Nelle. You know he—" But I cut off Harmony before she can finish.

"*Don't* 'come on, Nelle' me. I asked point blank for no one to contact a private investigator. It's like what I say regarding my own life doesn't matter to him." I snap back at her, waving an arm in Anthony's direction. "That's not how this works. That's not how *any* of this works."

I angle myself in Anthony's direction, "Anthony, since you can't respect my boundaries I'll make this easy for you." My next few words come out strikingly harsh, just as I intend for them to be, "Get out... NOW. And lose my number."

Anthony glances at me in surprise and then he looks toward Harmony for help. She intentionally avoids his direct eye contact as she pats him on the back and stands.

"Well, you heard the woman of the house," she says as she walks in the direction of the front door.

"Janelle, this is ridiculous! I come to you with information about some shit you asked us for but because it's not what you want to hear, you're pissed at *me!?*" he exclaims, throwing his arms up then raking both hands over his hair. What about what just happened? Did our kiss mean nothing to you?" Anthony asks, frustration clearly lined his face.

The silence that falls between us is deafening. He takes my silence as an answer before following Harmony to the front door. Just before he exits, he takes one final glance back at me.

"But I'm here if you ever need me," he adds before turning back to Harmony.

"I'm sorry, I'll talk to her." I hear Harmony say to him, "I'll call you later."

"Thanks. Talk soon." Anthony mutters with dismay as he exits my residence and walks toward his truck.

Chapter 8

Janelle

Harmony closes the door and practically jogs back to the living room. I already know what's coming as I pace the floor awaiting her return.

"Biiiiitch!" she exclaims, excitedly. "Y'all kissed? Ain't neither one of y'all told me a thing!"

I turn around with tear filled eyes, "Yes." I admit before allowing myself to become fully immersed by my emotions.

Tears stream down my face as I allow myself to experience everything I've been holding in. I feel myself collapse onto the couch, Harmony immediately reaches out to hold me and allows me to cry on her shoulder. My thoughts bombard me at once, my fears of becoming a widow before my daughter is born, her never knowing her father, single motherhood, Rosetta Hamilton, Anthony—the kiss. It all consumes my entire being. I feel as if I'm being pulled underwater by a monster of a wave, desperate for more air.

I cry out, "I can't do this! I can't be a mother by myself, I don't know what I'm doing! I need my parents here!" I pause, sitting myself upright for a moment to look Harmony in the eyes and say "I need my *husband, I need Percy!*"

I let out a wail so pain filled, I hardly recognize the sound coming from my mouth.

"It's okay, Hun. Let it all out" she says, rubbing a hand along my back and motioning for me to lay back on the couch. She continues "You and baby girl are gonna be just fine. I've got y'all. You're never alone as long as I'm here".

As minutes pass by, my sobs slowly begin to cease. By the time they stop completely I am pure exhausted. My eyelids have gradually grown heavier and heavier the more I seem to calm down from my breakdown. Eventually, I give in to the exhaustion as everything fades to darkness.

* * *

When I open my eyes everything appears somewhat hazy. I blink a few times, knowing how blurry my eyes can be when first waking up. It doesn't seem to help but I brush it off and tell myself that I'll grab the eye drops once I get to the bathroom. I sit up on the couch bringing my feet down onto the floor. Immediately, I'm lightheaded. I lower my head, pulling my chest down to my knees and take a couple deep breaths.

When I spot Harmony she's in my tan oversized recliner with the remote pointed at the TV. She turns the volume up as she reads the headline "Police Chief Delgado's 'Quality Mindset' Program a Success" aloud before noticing me.

Harmony turns her head mechanical like towards me before the rest of her body follows while repeating "Change Your Mindset". I can tell she's not herself because her eyes appear to be glazed over as she recites the phrase while gradually increasing in volume until the words are drumming loudly inside of my head.

This is a different type of feeling, it's as if that phrase is hypnotizing me. The floor slowly falls into a spiral before my eyes. Just as the lightheaded makes a return, the room starts to spin into total blackness.

* * *

"Be careful!!" says Harmony as I'm jolted awake after nearly falling off the couch during that bizarre dream. "Are you okay?"

"Yeah" I reply as I sit up, yawning and stretching my arms above my head. "My head is pounding though."

"I believe it. That was a *much needed* cry session you had there."

She walks over and gives me a hug.

"I just hate to see you hurting like this. But I bet you feel at least a little better now, don't you?"

"Somewhat, I think my emotional pain transformed into physical pain. My head is killing me," I answer while massaging my forehead.

"What'd your dad used to say?" She asks with a smirk.

I roll my eyes and repeat the phrase my dad always recited in response to my head hurting at any given time.

"If I had a head that big…" I pause allowing Harmony to join along. "My head would hurt too."

We burst out into a fit of laughter that shouldn't be as long winded as it is. It gets to a point that we're no longer laughing at my dad's phrase but at each other. Tears start to form in each of our eyes as our unintentional frenzy of howling laughter continues.

"Whew!" I exclaim minutes later, after Harmony and I have both regained our composures. "My stomach hurts from laughing so hard."

"I know it, mine too but I bet that headache is gone," Harmony says.

Disbelief floods my face as I realize it's gone, "You know what!? You're right!"

"I always am!" She says with a smirk, "So…"

I sigh "I know…you want the details."

"Yup, you know it."

I let out a slow exhale before beginning, "The kiss sort of just…

happened. I honestly don't know what came over me. First I was apologizing, then next thing I know my lips were on his."

"Well, how was it?" she asks, full of curiosity.

"It was amazing, almost as if his lips were meant just for mine." I blush a little, taking a throw pillow into my grasp and squeezing it tight. "But it was a mistake. I have zero tolerance when it comes to disrespecting my boundaries."

Harmony lets out a sigh "I feel you there. When he told me about the PI, I had no idea that he hadn't discussed it with you yet."

"It's cool but there are some things I'd like to keep on the low. I don't think he realizes how embarrassing all of this is for me. I mean seriously, I'm finding out some of the most embarrassing details of my life right now. I don't want him to know how pitiful my marriage actually was."

"Wow... I didn't really think of it in that way, Nelle," says Harmony. "Please know that you have nothing to be embarrassed about though. You were a perfect wife to Percy and if he was in fact cheating then he holds all the blame and embarrassment."

"That's easier said than done."

"I know it girl, I know..." she trails off before continuing "I do wonder what that PI told Anthony although I don't feel like it's too much of anything or else he would've told me the overall jist of it while talking yesterday."

"I don't want any more information about my life coming from Anthony and I'd appreciate it, if you'd refrain from discussing my marriage with him too." I say to Harmony.

"Of course, my bad girl."

"I don't mind your help though, you're my sister. You know me in and out and you've always been there for me and vice versa. And I would like to get to the bottom of this. It's not too late to take you up on your social media investigator friend, is it?" I question, hoping I don't have to plead with her.

"Oh girl! Definitely! She'll have everything figured out within a week, if not sooner," Harmony says with excitement. "She's also a psychic. Whether you need her detective skills or her psychic skills, my girl gotcha."

I've always been someone that is skeptical of people who claim to see the future or talk to the dead. In one instance, I would love to contact Percy from the spirit realm but I ain't trying to bring anything malevolent into my life.

This could be my chance to get some answers about Percy, I think to myself but I'm not taking any chances with that stuff so I force myself to push the thought away.

"Chile, you know I'm scary! I ain't about to have no demon trying to sacrifice my life for its gain!" I sass back at her, "I know how those movies end."

Harmony laughs and says "Let me hit her up now, I guarantee by this time tomorrow, she'll have information faster than any PI you could hire."

"I'm fine with that. If you trust her, then I do too," I agree. "I'm gonna grab some water first, my throat feels kind of parched."

"Parched?!" exclaims Harmony. "Since when did you start using words like *parched?*"

I burst out laughing, not bothering to answer her question as I stand to get an ice cold glass of water from the kitchen.

I can hear Harmony dialing numbers on her phone as I enter the kitchen. I pull a clean glass down from the cabinet, rinse it out and press the glass under my ice maker. I switch the ice type to crushed and proceed to fill my glass with iced water.

I take a sip while glancing out the kitchen window as I begin to recall that strange dream. *What was that phrase Harmony kept repeating? Be the Change? Change Your Mind? Change Your Mindset!*

Finally the police department has created a pathway to attempt to bridge the gap between their officers and our youth. *But is that an actual program or just something my mind created in my dream?*

The lines between what is real and what I've dreamt get mixed up a lot. It's mainly due to the fact that a lot of my dreams come true in some way or shape. For instance, I've had recurring dreams of a past partner's infidelity, only to find out he was cheating with the exact person I saw him with in those dreams.

"Hey Nelle, come here. I've got Izzy on the phone," says Harmony as she takes a seat at my kitchen table, withdrawing me from my thoughts.

I pull out the chair I was sitting in just hours ago with Anthony and listen with eager ears.

"Janelle, I've got Isabella here. If you could just tell her what information you would like her to know, she can get started on helping you find some answers." Harmony explains to me while handing over her phone.

I put the phone on speaker so that she can hear also and introduce myself to Isabella.

"Hi Isabella, I'm Janelle. Harmony has told me your detective skills are unmatched."

Isabella laughs, "I mean, not to toot my own horn but she's not lying! And please, call me Izzy, Isabella makes me feel like I'm about to be scolded."

"Izzy, it is then", I reply. "So long story short, my husband recently passed away in an automobile accident, a woman was reported as being in the truck with him but leaving the site before the ambulance and police arrived. At his funeral site, I believe that same woman was present and I'm wanting to find out everything I can about her."

"I'm so sorry about your loss, Janelle, just know, you are not alone. Do you have any information such as her name or age?" asks Izzy.

"Well, I found out from one of my husband's coworkers that he had been seen having intimate conversations with an inmate that was recently released. Her name is Rosetta Hamilton," I explain. "I've got her most recent contact information but that's it."

"Does that include her inmate number?" questions Izzy.

"Yes, that's 16009," I answer.

"Okay, is there anything else you know?"

"No, this is all. Is that enough info to find anything out?" I ask.

"Well," says Izzy, "it's a start. What's your number so I can call you as soon as possible with any updates?"

We exchange numbers and say our goodbyes with a promise to have new details about Rosetta Hamilton within the next 24 hours.

Chapter 9

Anthony

I *can't ever seem to do anything right*, I think to myself as my truck crawls to a stop in front of my apartment building.

I could tell by the way Janelle looked at me with such hatred in her eyes that I've fucked up terribly this time. I can't seem to think of a way to get back on her good side.

I kick off my shoes at the front door as I enter my place. I walk through the living room towards the kitchen to wash my hands, grab a beer from the fridge then lazily flop down in my recliner.

But there's no way in hell I'm giving up that easily. Janelle doesn't know who she's met. It's gonna take a lot more to get rid of me. I think to myself.

I'll have to talk Harmony into making Janelle realize she needs me. Although, maybe I'm the idiot for thinking Harmony wouldn't mention the private detective. *Good thing there isn't one*, I think to myself. Either way, now I know when it comes to Janelle, Harmony won't hesitate to throw me under the bus.

I'll tell Harmony that Rosetta reached out to me, returning a message I previously left for her and she wants to meet with Janelle. She'll go back, persuade Janelle to agree and I'll be back in her good graces.

"That'll work!" I say aloud before taking another sip of my Beck's beer, grinning to myself at my clever plan.

I decide it will be best to go ahead and contact Rosetta. Reaching for my phone, I unlock it then dial her number. It rings only twice before she picks up.

"Hello?" she answers when she picks up.

I pause a second before deciding how to respond. I didn't expect her to pick up the phone but I need Rosetta and Janelle so this is a risk I'm willing to accept.

"Hello Ms Hamilton, this is Correctional Officer Miller from FCI Fairfield. Are you available to sit down with Janelle Williams, Warden Williams' wife? I was told you have been wanting to speak with her." I usher out quickly but it's not quick enough as I hear the line disconnect.

The abrupt ending to our call surprised me, to say the least. *I'll have to think of a plan B,* I think to myself as my phone dings with a new text message.

Opening it, I realize it's from Rosetta's number.

Rosetta: Yes. Meet me Saturday at five p.m. at my residence.

Hell yeah! Original plan is back on track! I burst with excitement as adrenaline flows throughout my body.

Chapter 10

Janelle

Twenty hours have passed since I spoke to Izzy and I haven't heard back from her yet. It makes me question her reliability because if she's as good as Harmony says she is, wouldn't she already have *some type* of information?

To keep my mind occupied, I sit down with a few snacks to watch the newest episode of 'CSI'. Nothing eases my mind like solving a case before the actors can. I'm about 40 minutes into the episode when my phone rings, it's Harmony.

"Hey girl," I say as I pick up, pressing pause on my remote so I don't miss the beginning of the next show.

"Hey Nelle, what are you up to? Have you heard from Anthony? Has Izzy got back up with you, yet? What did she find?" She drills at me, question after question.

"Damn, why the interrogation?" I laugh in response.

"Just answer my questions, girl!" Harmony retorts.

"I'm finishing up an episode of CSI I started earlier. I haven't spoken to Anthony, I hope it stays that way. And no, I haven't talked to Izzy yet."

"Oh yeah? What's the episode about? So you're still upset with Ant, huh?" She asks.

"Honestly, I don't care to ever have his name brought up around me again. You know a person not respecting my boundaries is an automatic cut off," I answer. "But as for the episode, it's the newest one where there are identical twin sisters and one commits murder but has the other one framed. You wanna know how it ends?" I ask before continuing.

Harmony thinks it over for a second before saying "Go ahead, I probably won't get to it any time soon."

"Well the twin that committed the murder almost got away with it due to identical twins having the same DNA but ultimately it came down to fingerprints. Apparently, even though identical twins share the same DNA, their fingerprints are still unique to each person so they were able to arrest the correct twin for the murder."

"Oh shit, that really gives a new meaning to the phrase "evil twin," she laughs. "There's always some truth to all those old phrases."

I give a small chuckle, "Have you heard from Ant?" I ask although unsure of why I care to know.

79

"Actually yeah, he called me last night to tell me that he reached out to Ros before your big blow up with him. He said that they discussed you two meeting to talk about everything you want to know." She pauses briefly then continues "Would that be something you're willing to do?"

Immediately, I feel my heart rate increase and am aware of my blood pulsing through my veins. Taking a deep breath, I exhale slowly before answering.

The thought of Anthony makes me roll my eyes, "He could've just dropped everything like I asked... but I guess if I truly want answers, I will need to speak with her."

"So that's a yes? Just want to make sure before letting Anthony know." She hesitates before carrying on, "I *can* let him know, right?"

"You can give him the go ahead to set it up. Find out what day, what time and the location I can meet her at."

"Perfect! I'll call him as soon as we hang up."

"One more thing Harmony, please tell him he needs to stay out of my business after this. I don't want to have to keep repeating myself." I say.

Harmony gives a loud sigh.

"What? What is it?" I ask her.

"I mean, you don't think it's best for Anthony to be there with us? Neither one of us knows this woman, she could have ulterior motives." She insists with sternness.

I stand for a moment then walk over to a window to open it for some fresh air before answering.

"Hell nah!" I reply a bit too loudly into my phone. "Anthony has done more than enough."

"Are you sure though, Nelle? I mean she is an ex con."

I have to admit, this is something I didn't really think about. I only took into account that she's an older woman and assumed she'd be safe enough to meet woman to woman.

"Let me think about it before I make any definite decisions on whether I want him with us or not."

"Just use your logic about this, not your emotions and let me know either way. I'll go ahead and give Anthony a call back so he can get the time, date and all that good stuff set up."

"Sounds good. If he asks whether he can come or not, just tell him no for now." I say into the receiver before glancing down at my phone as another call beeps through.

"Hey Har, I better grab this call, it's Izzy. Keep your fingers crossed she has some useful information for me. I'll talk to you right after, k? Love you, bye!" I say before clicking over to the other call.

"Hi Izzy!" I answer cheerfully.

"Janelle, hi! I'm just calling with an update like I said I would," she replies.

My mouth goes completely dry, anxiousness flooding me.

"That's... ahem," I say, clearing my throat, "that's great, so let's hear it."

"Well, I was hoping I could meet you at home or somewhere in town to show you a few things concerning what I've found."

Oh shit! Has she found actual evidence of an affair? I think, pacing in place before heading towards the full length mirror in my bedroom to see how I look.

"Umm– Yeah, sure. Let's meet because my house isn't up for 'company' standards right now." I give a slight laugh out of nervousness. "How about we meet at The Chew?"

"That works for me" Izzy replies. "Should I say in about two hours?"

"That's cool." I respond, "See you soon!"

* * *

After hopping in the shower and spritzing my hair with water to liven it up some, I slide my legs into some army green leggings and throw on a fitted, black maternity top. I walk over to my closet, grabbing my black and white Converses before stopping by my jewelry stand. Spotting my signature clear quartz necklace, I quickly fasten it around my neck. I throw on a small bit of foundation and spray my face with setting spray after filling in my eyebrows to perfection. Finally, I'm fully dressed and ready to leave the house.

The drive over is beautiful. This time of year is always my favorite due to the changing color of leaves and the crisp fall air. It reminds me of my childhood and playing in the many piles of leaves my dad raked in our yard. The memory makes me smile but brings on a feeling of loneliness that I can't shake.

I'm a ball of nerves as I pull into the parking lot because I'm not at all sure what to expect. I practice the 5-4-3-2-1 grounding technique I learned while in therapy to calm me a little before exiting my vehicle.

I arrive a few minutes early so the hostess seats me at an inside booth and let me know my waitress will be right over. I tell her there's no rush since I'm meeting someone and I'd like to wait on them.

Not even five minutes go by before I see a Hispanic woman walking over to my table. She has an average build, looks to be about 5'5" and has shoulder length dark hair. She's wearing black pants with a black and white flannel top.

"Are you Janelle?" she asks.

"Yup, that's me!" I reply cheerfully, "You must be Izzy."

"The one and only," Izzy replies as she takes a seat across the booth from me.

Once she's settled in her seat, she gets straight to business.

"I've learned quite a bit of information about Rosetta Hamilton," she says while pulling her laptop along with a couple papers from her bag.

I lean forward with intrigue. "And...?"

"And, she was arrested for kidnapping and child endangerment. She wasn't arrested until the late 90's due to her daughter becoming pregnant and passing away during childbirth."

"Kidnapping!? I never would've guessed based on her photo." I say, "How exactly did she end up with the child endangerment charge?"

"Her daughter's pregnancy was due to Rosetta allowing her to be sexually and emotionally abused."

"She allowed people to sexually abuse her own daughter!?" I question in disbelief, suddenly feeling sick to my stomach.

Humans never cease to amaze me. I don't understand how anyone, let alone a *mother,* could willingly allow anyone to abuse their own flesh and blood.

Just as Izzy is about to answer, a plump, blonde haired twenty-something year old waitress greets us.

"Hi, my name is Jessica and I'll be your server today. What can I get y'all to drink?", she inquired in a chipper voice.

"Hi, I'd like a water please," I reply.

"And for you?" she asks, turning towards Izzy.

"I'll take a water also," says Izzy.

"Got it, do you know what you want to eat or do you need a few minutes?" Jessica asks.

I glance over at Izzy for a response due to the fact that I usually get one of three entrees when I come here.

"I'm ready to order if you are," I say to her.

"Actually, I won't be here long. I just would like a glass of water please," Izzy answers.

I didn't expect to come here for food either but with the way my baby girl is so active I'm pretty sure she's telling me she wants food. *She's a bossy little thing and ain't even here yet.*

"Okay, well what can I get you?" The waitress asks, turning her attention back to me.

"I'll take a half order of chicken nachos to go please." I answer, mouth already salivating at the taste.

"Anything else?"She asks while jotting down my order.

"That'll be it." I reply with a smile.

"Got it! I'll get this order put in and I'll be right back with your waters."

Once Jessica leaves our table I turn my attention back to Izzy.

"So, back to my question. Rosetta allowed someone to take advantage of her daughter?" I ask.

"It was a messy case. The accused abuser was reportedly her own son. He was close in age to her daughter. I'm not sure whether they were related by blood or due to the kidnapping but with a little more time I am positive I can figure that part out as well.

"Do you have their names? Location? Phone numbers?" I inquire.

I don't have her daughter's name…*yet* but I did find out that her son's name is DeAndre Hamilton," she says.

I think for a minute of any DeAndre's I may know but come up blank.
    "And do you know whether DeAndre has been in contact with Rosetta recently?"

"I don't have that information. It's almost as if he disappeared from the face of the planet," she continues. "The case was messy due to the fact that she wouldn't testify. There's also something involving her and a homicide but I'm finding it difficult to find any information on it. I'm not sure if those records could've been expunged or what."

"So she may have committed a murder, kidnappings and now she's back on the street? How is that possible?" I wonder aloud.

"Apparently, good behavior is awarded very generously in our prison system nowadays," she replies, startling me momentarily due to not knowing she heard me. "Supposedly, there was a child born from the rape of her daughter by her son however, I can't seem to find much information on that right now."

I lean back as Jessica comes back with our waters and a basket of chips and salsa.

86

"Thank you," I say as she sets our glasses down on the table.

"No problem! I'll have your to-go plate out shortly," she says gleefully, leaving us to ourselves.

Directing my attention back to Izzy, I say "Wow, this is a lot." I feel a wave of nausea roll throughout my body but I brush it off as best as I can. "My frie– my ex friend," I catch and correct myself. "My husband's coworker, Anthony, has been in communication with Rosetta. I'm planning to sit down and get some answers about her and Percy."

Izzy displays a confused look on her face before responding, "Why would an ex friend be doing this for you?"

"Well, it's a long story but to keep it short, he was helping me find information on Rosetta. Much like you are but he kept overstepping his boundaries when it came to details of my life." I hesitate before continuing, "I'd be lying if I said I didn't miss his friendship though."

"Sometimes friendships are for a lifetime and other times they're only for a season." She takes a sip of water then continues, "But what's meant to be, will be. So you're gonna meet up with her? I guess you probably won't need me anymore since you're going directly to the source."

"Yeah, I guess you're right," I say aloud, barely audible before I continue. "I tend to take broken friendships harder than my past relationships. I only consider the relationship I had with my husband to be a *real* relationship, all the others were puppy love relationships."

A flashback of the first time Percy and I kissed has me in a hold for a moment. We were leaving the late movie showing of *'The Wood'*. I was thrilled because he knew how much I loved Taye Diggs. Once we were settled in his beat up old Honda Accord, we sat there talking about everything imaginable under the moonlight. I can still imagine his eager, boy-like smile right before he licked his lips, reminding me of LL Cool J, then leaned towards me, pulling my face to his.

I shake away the memory before continuing, "But yeah, I think I'm going to talk with Rosetta. I'm hoping she'll shoot it to me straight with no bullshit. I just want to know the truth about her and my husband."

Izzy tilts her head and smiles, glancing from me to slightly behind me and back.

"You have so much love for your husband, I can literally feel it radiating off of you!" She exclaims, remaining silent very briefly then saying "He's got just as much for you."

Izzy closes her eyes, lowers her head and releases a big exhale. "It's such an amazing feeling but it's almost overwhelming," she says, opening her tear filled eyes and smiling.

It catches me off guard but Izzy must be communicating with Percy as we sit here. I momentarily forgot that Harmony said Izzy is also a psychic.

"Wait, what? He's here now!?" I ask with unnerving excitement.

Izzy gives a chuckle, "He's in the vicinity, He hasn't shown himself to me yet but I can feel him. He–" she halts.

Seriousness crosses her face as she stares off behind me, in the distance for an unusually longer than normal amount of time.

This starts to worry me. Questions begin to flood my mind, *What just happened? Is it not really Percy? Is Izzy screwing with me?*

"Izzy," I mutter, frightened and confused. "Izzy, are you okay?" I ask while waving a hand in front of her face.

She quickly snaps out of her trance, "Oh. What was that?"

"Are you okay? You stopped during the middle of your sentence and were staring off into space just now."

"Oh my gosh, I'm so sorry. When I'm channeling spirits, sometimes they'll want to get their message across so badly that their voices eventually begin to block out all other distractions."

At that very moment, Jessica walks over to deliver my to-go plate. She holds it out with a smile on her face.

"Here's your to-go nachos. Can I get y'all anything else?"

"No, thank you. The check is fine." I answer with a fake smile, still unsure how to feel about what just happened. All I know is I want to leave.

Jessica pulls a black booklet from her apron pocket and hands it to me.

"I thought you might say that, I brought it over anyway," she says, leaving the booklet with me and walking away.

I flip open the book, preparing myself for the damage, $8.47. *That's not bad at all.* I pull out a 10 dollar and 5 dollar bills, inserting them into the black booklet before placing it on the table.

Intrigued, I direct my attention back to our conversation before Jessica interrupted. "That's pretty wild. I imagine it's tough having your own inner thoughts as well as those of the non living."

Izzy chuckles, shaking her head from side to side quickly and says, "Trust me, they're living alright! Just because he isn't present in this physical realm doesn't mean he's no longer living. But no, it's more like someone very lightly knocking on a door to get my attention and if I don't notice it soon enough, they'll start banging and shouting at me until I do."

"Well, what did he say?" I ask genuinely curious for the first time.

"He was showing me a letter but I didn't get a good chance to study it so I could fully make it out. It was a letter, either a D or the top part of a R."

"Maybe it was both and he's telling me I deserve a vacation to the Dominican Republic," I joke in an attempt to brush off the uneasiness I still feel. "But it could be for DeAndre or Rosetta".

Seriousness sets in on Izzy again.

"...Izzy...What is it?" I question her softly.

There's no acknowledgment that she hears my words. Instantly, I'm spooked again and just ready to get out of there.

"Izzy, you're scaring me. I'm gonna head out," I say as I grab my purse, standing to leave. I take exactly three steps before I hear Izzy call out my name.

"Janelle..." she says, "I just got another message. He says to *Be careful.*"

How ominous is that? Hearing a message like that from a so-called spirit is terrifying. Unsure how to reply, I nod my head towards her then turn, exiting the building.

Chapter 11

Janelle

I high tail it out of the parking lot faster than I've ever seen any pregnant woman move. I can't help it, I'm a bit more shaken up than I thought I would be. I mean seriously, Izzy kind of spring all that paranormal shit on me.

I travel across town in what has to be a record time because I can't even recall the drive. However, that could be due to the fact that I start feeling an intense amount of pressure in my abdomen.

It feels like menstrual cramps, only with a bit more intensity to them. *How the hell are first time moms supposed to know the difference between Braxton Hicks contractions and the real ones?*

I pull into my driveway, throw the car into park then lean back against my seat with a big exhale. *Why would Izzy do that?! If I had known that she channels messages from the dead without warning, I would have decided against our meet up.* I take a couple deep breaths, trying my hardest to compose myself. However, it does little to minimize the terrifying thoughts running through my mind.

I have never been one to mess around with the spirit world and I wasn't planning to begin. I'm kicking myself because I've always been told to stay away from all that especially while pregnant as some malevolent entities sometimes tries to enter the body of your unborn child.

My mind begins spiraling as I overthink the possibility of whatever spirit Izzy was talking to trying to hurt my baby. *Could that be the reason for the pain I just felt? More importantly, who's to say it was real or not? And if it was, how would I know it's really Percy?*

After sitting in my car decompressing for a few more minutes, I decide I'm not ready to be alone so text Harmony to let her know I'm on my way over.

My phone pings just as I pull out onto one of the long county roads that leads to her house.

"Okay, let yourself in." She texts back.

I give a thumbs up reaction to her message and toss my phone into the passenger seat. I push the volume button on my steering wheel to hear the song on the radio but immediately turn it back off.

The song playing is *Spend My Life* by Eric Benét and Tamia, it was one of mine and Percy's first slow dances together as husband and wife.

But I can't afford to get lost in thought about our wedding night right now though. I have to fill Harmony in on what just happened.

The longer I think back on the apparent message from Percy, the more I'm starting to believe it's him. *Be careful,* I think to myself. *Could this be a sign that I should allow Anthony to tag along when I speak to Rosetta?*

Before I can ruminate on that possibility any further, Harmony's home comes into view. It's just my luck that Anthony's white truck is here also.

I should have known he'd be here.

Surprisingly, I'm okay with him being present today. I feel like this is further confirmation that I'm understanding Percy's message correctly but just to be sure I begin pleading, "Come on P, give me something solid," in hopes of receiving a very obvious sign from him.

Of course Harmony is being logical in suggesting that Anthony should be there when dealing with a former federal inmate. It's true, we don't know what she's capable of. However, I'm not too sure if Anthony knows either considering she was released within the first week or so of his employment at the prison but surely he knows how to handle things should they escalate.

I cut the ignition to my car, stepping out of my vehicle only to be hit by an overwhelming scent of cedar, leather and tobacco with a soft hint of jasmine. It's a scent I recognize immediately, Tom Ford Ombré Eau de Parfum. I know this because it was one of Percy's signature colognes and one of my favorites for him to wear.

Confirmation? I'll take it.

I side-step past Anthony and Harmony's vehicles, wobbling my way to the front door. I ring the doorbell, give my special knock and enter the code to let myself in.

"Harmony, it's me!" I shout.

"We're in here," she yells back from the living room.

I hesitate for a second to decide if I want Anthony knowing about what just happened with Izzy before making my way towards them.

"Hey Nelle" Harmony says as soon as I enter.

"Hey Harmony...Ant" I reply while glancing at Anthony and quickly looking away.

He offers a small smile and a soft head nod.

"You okay?" Harmony questions as concern slowly consumes her face. "You look a bit shaken, like you've seen or *spoken* to a ghost!" she says with a mischievous side smirk.

"Actually, that's exactly what happened. It scared the shit out of me, no lie," I reply, probably a little too dramatically.

I decided it's safe to keep Anthony *'in the know'* since I'm hoping he'll agree to come with us to meet Rosetta. I know I'm probably not on his list of favorite people right now but maybe I can get back on his good side.

Horror spreads across Harmony's face, "My girl didn't show out now, did she?"

"If by *show out*, you mean channel messages from the dead...then yeah. Yeah, she did," I retort satirically. "She scared me so bad I thought I was having contractions!"

"Chile, I don't know what to do with her! I've told her not to spring that kind of thing on people. You never know if they're open to hearing those types of things."

"She just ain't come 'cross the right person yet." Anthony inserts matter of factly as he turns his attention towards me, "But Nelle, I can't sit here and act like shit is cool after how everything ended the other day. Damn, a nigga don't even know how to act around you."

The sudden roughness of his tone sends excitement through my veins. *A man taking authority is such a turn on*, I can't help but think.

Harmony looks over at him quickly with an eyebrow raised and shock on her face before directing her attention back to me. "And he said what he said," she adds with a snap of her fingers with a laugh.

"Anthony, I don't blame you if you can't forgive me and don't want anything to do with me," I begin, "and I do want you in my life. I would actually love your help with all of this but the one thing I refuse to back down on are my boundaries."

He eases closer to me, reaching for my hands. Suddenly, it's as if he and I are the only ones in the room.

He gazes into my soul with purpose as he says, barely audible "You got a nigga getting soft." He leans his forehead down to mine, smiles and adds, "It takes more than that to get rid of me."

There's something about the way he said that last sentence that doesn't sit just right with me. I can't put a finger on it but there was something off about it.

I don't get a chance to dwell on it any longer because I hear one of our phones start to buzz.

I grab my phone quickly to see who is calling, it's Izzy on FaceTime. *What else could she want right now?* I wonder but reluctantly, I answer.

"Hi Izzy, I'm here with Harmony and Anthony," I say hoping she picks up on the fact that he's the coworker of Percy's that we discussed earlier. "Anything new?" I question.

"Hey Janelle, hey y'all," she replies as Harmony and Anthony each lean into the camera frame to wave back. "No, not yet. I'm calling because I wanted to make sure you were okay. You left in a hurry once I started channeling Percy's messages. I know that sort of thing can freak some people out so I just wanted to check on you."

"Yeah, you asked so Imma be honest. The way all that happened back at The Chew wasn't cool. You gotta let people know beforehand about the way you channel spirits unexpectedly, so they can choose whether they're prepared to hear the message. I don't even know you, if we're being honest."

I could continue but decide not to fuss her out too badly considering I could possibly still need her help.

"Girl, you done scared my good sis half to death!" Harmony exclaims, leaning forward into the frame again.

"My apologies, this is so embarrassing. It's almost as if they hold me hostage until the message is relayed," she explains remorsefully. "I also meant to ask while we were together, but would you be open to a private investigator friend of mine helping me?"

I respond immediately "No, that's—"

"That's what I wanna know about" says Harmony, snatching the phone from my hands and panning it over towards Anthony so that Izzy can see him. "What were you saying about a PI earlier?" she questions him.

Anthony seems caught off guard once the camera finds him. Meanwhile, Izzy awaits his response with a look I can't seem to quite figure out.

"Are you originally from around here, Anthony?" Izzy quizzes him.

"I'm actually from—" but he's interrupted by his own ringing phone. He glances down at the caller and quickly excuses himself. "It's the new warden, I've got to take this."

That statement sends a knife hurling directly into my heart. I know companies have to replace people and the positions they held but it still hurts to hear mention of a new warden. Percy should still be holding that title.

"We'll find all that out and fill you in. If you get any more info let me know." I say after grabbing my phone from Harmony.

Izzy has that serious look on her face once again, the same exact one she had in the restaurant earlier.

"Janelle, can I tell you something without upsetting you?" she asks.

"I mean that depends on what it is." I reply with an unsure smile.

"I don't want to freak you out but there's a darkness close to you. Please take your husband's advice and be careful. Someone is plotting against you so please use caution when meeting with Rosetta."

"No worries, I'm not planning on doing any of this alone." I reassure her before adding, "And thanks, but no thanks to the PI." We say our good-bye's just before ending the call.

Chapter 12

Janelle

Anthony enters the house again after he's hung up from his call. I'm curious to know who it is since it was so important that he needed to leave the house. Instead I choose to find out what this private investigator told him.

"Good, you're back. So what did your PI friend find out?" I ask.

"I don't even know if I should answer this," he replies sarcastically.

Touché, I admit to myself, I kind of deserve that.

I give a soft chuckle, "Yeah, I had that coming."

Anthony's eyes twinkle playfully, softening once he realizes I'm smirking, making it a struggle to stay upset at.

"Not anything new really...just that Rosetta still has a living child," he answers.

"Right, Izzy found that out as well. We know that the living adult child's name is DeAndré Hamilton." I nod my head in agreement, "That's actually why I was rushing over here. I wanted to fill Harmony in on this new information... And well, now you know too."

Anthony gulps down his beer before asking "And where is he? Could Percy have known them from back in the day, maybe they grew up together? I mean that may explain why he was so close to Rosetta."

My heart starts to flutter at the fact that Anthony is even considering another possibility. This definitively lets me know he didn't intend to offend me.

"Good point, I hadn't thought of that," I answer. "It makes me feel better to think that may have been the case."

"Rosetta could set all of this straight," interrupts Harmony. "Have you had a chance to speak with her again, Ant?"

"Umm... Yeah. I actually did speak to her, is five o'clock pm, Saturday at her place in Howie, okay?"

My face scrunches up at the thought of meeting her at her place but before I can object Anthony continues explaining.

"Hol' up! Let me finish," he says as he holds up his hand, silencing me. "You have to realize she is a recently released inmate. She doesn't have the same freedoms and liberties we have to meet wherever she'd like. She's allowed access to so few places that it would be easier to go to her."

"Okay, fine." I say while throwing my hands up to concede without protest. "I don't care where I have to meet her as long as you can come with us…" I decide out loud. "Harmony made a lot of sense the other day mentioning it would be best to have you present..you know. Just in case Rosetta tries to kill us or something."

"Yeah, she definitely had a reputation in prison. With age she apparently became more laid back but I've heard a number of ridiculous stories about her during her youth" says Anthony. "I was damn sho going to volunteer myself to come with y'all just for the added security in case shit goes left."

He looks over to Harmony then licks his lips and rubs his hands together like that one Birdman GIF as he continues. "But it looks like Harmony put in a good word for me" he says with a wink towards Harmony and proceeds to dap her up like she's one of the boys.

"I wasn't doing yo ass any favors!" She laughs, "I was just tryna make sure my black ass stays safe!"

I can't help but burst into a fit of laughter along with Anthony.

"Y'all laughing, but I'm serious. Shit. One thing Imma always make sure of is that I'm safe!" Harmony finishes with humor all on her face.

"Where exactly is Howie?" I ask after settling down from laughter.

"It's not too far," says Anthony. "Bout a forty-five minute drive. If you blink too long you'll miss the entire town, though."

"Yeah, it's a really small country town," pipes up Harmony. "I didn't think black people live there, though. I could've sworn somebody told me it's a sundown town."

"So we gotta watch out for white folks as well as Rosetta!?" I shake my head in disbelief.

"Shit, I forgot we have *Worrisome Wendy* over here," she says while walking over to her record player and placing a vinyl record on it.

"I'm just saying, it sounds like this place is in the middle of nowhere. What if something…happens?" I trail off while imagining worst case scenarios in my mind.

Next thing I know, I hear Kendrick Lamar's voice rapping "We gon' be aight."

"You're an ass!" I exclaim with a laugh while tossing a hunter green throw pillow at her.

I can always count on Harmony to relieve tension with something hilarious up her sleeves. She lowers the volume, allowing the album play in the background as she walks back over to us after scooping up the pillow.

"But seriously y'all, I can forget everything if this could be dangerous." I say bringing our attention back to the topic.

Anthony grabs my hand in his, kisses it and looks into my eyes, "You are going to be perfectly fine, I got you."

My entire body becomes engulfed in a sudden flame rising from within my core as he squeezes my hand. The certainty in his words along with the confidence in his tone makes me a bit embarrassed by where my thoughts go. *I wonder if he takes control like this in all situations...*

I imagine us lying in bed after rounds of amazing sex with our fingers entwined together while I listen to his steadily slowing heartbeat as my head rests on his chest. But I hardly get a chance to enjoy my daydream due to Harmony interrupting it.

"Yeah girl, we'll be fine but what the hell were you just thinking about?!" She questions with a smirk as she looks back and forth between the two of us.

"Girl, boo!" I laugh as I sense heat rushing to my cheeks. "Anyways, so Saturday? As in next weekend?"

"No, as in tomorrow," answers Anthony after glancing at his Apple Watch for the date. "I intended to ask you earlier this week but I kind of wasn't given the opportunity to do so."

I feel so ashamed about shutting Anthony down before he was able to fully explain himself so I feel obligated to agree to this last minute arrangement. This could be my only chance to speak with Rosetta while she's willing to. I pray I get the answers I desperately want about my husband.

"Yeah... about that. I'm sorry again Anthony. But sure, I can make tomorrow at five work." I reply. "Who's driving?"

"I can," says Anthony. "We can meet at your house around 3:30 to give us plenty of time to get there and find her house."

"Sounds like a plan!" Harmony agrees, "Just know Imma come packing!"

"Lord, don't hurt nobody," I exclaim while rolling my eyes and cracking up.

"Nelle, you never told us exactly what Izzy channeled..." Harmony trails off as she realizes it may be something I don't want Anthony to know. "Oh, but it's aight if you want to keep that to yourself."

"Oh no, it's fine. Well, Izzy and I were talking and next thing I know she's staring off into space. At times, it seemed like she would look at me but not really at me. It was as if she was staring through me or something." I give a slight shiver as I notice goosebumps rising on my arms as I describe her strange behavior. "I kept calling her name to draw her attention back to me but I don't think she could hear me. So I told her I was freaked out and leaving."

"So she didn't actually relay a message from Percy?" Anthony asks, clearly puzzled.

"No, she did! She stopped me right before I walked away and said that Percy told her to tell me to *Be careful*. She also mentioned he was showing some letter but she was unable to make it out clearly, she's pretty sure it was either a D or an R."

I can tell the wheels turning in Harmony's head by the look on her face.

"Well, it's gotta have something to do with Rosetta or possibly her son DeAndré. Maybe we should meet elsewhere." Harmony suggests with concerned eyes. "How ironic is it that Izzy channels that message the day before we meet with this woman?"

"Look, everything is going to be fine. I'll be there and you've got to remember this is a woman that I've dealt with before." Anthony quickly adds, "She's nothing that I can't handle."

"I'm sure you can but maybe we should let someone else know we're going to meet her." I say with uncertainty.

I see Anthony's face transform into one of frustration when I glance his way.

"Man, hell nah! Either y'all gone let me protect y'all like a man should or you can get someone else to go," he shouts, clearly irritated.

I'm startled by his sudden outburst but in order to keep the peace, I quickly reply with "Okay, whatever. It's fine. Anyways, that was basically all that was said."

"Hmm..." Harmony thinks out loud, "So have you thought about what you're going to say to her?"

"Hell everything! Who is she? Who was she to Percy? What was she wanting Percy to tell me in those texts?"

"I feel you. This might be a lot to handle all at once, you sure you're good?" She questions, waiting for my response.

"I'm less than 24 hours away from finding out the truth about my husband. I'm fine." I assure her with a sincere smile and add, "Thank you for asking though."

Harmony turns to Anthony with a smirk, "See? This is what it looks like to respect boundaries."

He laughs then states flatly, "I'll remember who *not* to protect since you got jokes."

The tone of his voice makes it seem as if he's serious about it. I'm not sure I like the way this conversation is going and apparently neither does Harmony. She rolls her eyes so hard I'm afraid they may get stuck, then she looks down at her phone, checking the time.

"Well, I don't know where y'all are gonna go but y'all are 'bout to get the hell up out of here because I have a dick appointment that I have to get ready for."

Somewhat stunned by the sudden revelation that Harmony is seeing someone new and hasn't told me anything about it, I suddenly understand the unspoken words I read across her face. There's something she isn't saying, but she must not want Anthony to hear.

I nod in acknowledgment of reading between the lines and stand, grabbing my keys while Anthony does the same.

"I don't think I've ever been kicked out of anyone's house as much as you two kick me out," he says, standing and tossing his empty beer bottle in the trash along the way.

We say our goodbyes as Harmony walks us out.

"I'll see y'all tomorrow at 3:30," Anthony calls out of his window as he pulls out of Harmony's driveway.

I give a honk and wave as I follow behind him in the same direction, impatiently awaiting a phone call from Harmony.

Before I'm even thirty seconds down the road, my phone rings through my car speakers and Siri announces that Harmony is calling over my Apple CarPlay system.

Chapter 13

Janelle

"What the hell is wrong with Anthony?!" I hear Harmony say immediately through my speakers when I answer the call.

I have to admit, he hasn't really been his normal self lately. I thought it was just me overthinking as usual but if Harmony is thinking the same thing, I know it's him and not me.

"I'm not sure but he's been acting off lately. I thought I was being paranoid but if you're thinking the same thing then, maybe it's not me."

"He lowkey pissed me off saying he isn't going to protect me, what type of man says that?" She exclaims a bit too loudly, hurting my ears in the process. I lower the volume in my car before responding.

"He was probably just joking around," I say casually because I know if I get Harmony's mind thinking like mine we won't ever get around to speaking to Rosetta. "I don't see why telling anyone else about our plans would cause his outrage, though. I mean, it's always better to be safe than sorry."

"Mmhm…exactly my thoughts," agrees Harmony.. "I think we should still let someone know what our plans for tomorrow are."

"Well, maybe we better tell your dick appointment about it." I say sarcastically, hoping this will change the direction of the conversation. I'm literally itching to find out who this guy is and why she hasn't told me anything about him.

"Chile, I was just making up some shit to get Ant out of here because his smart ass mouth pissed me off. You know how I get when folks rub me the wrong way and I ain't tryna get like that right now."

"So there's no dick appointment tonight?" I ask, relieved to know my best friend isn't keeping things from me.

"Girl, nah but I wish! I feel like the old lady from the Titanic movie, *It's been 84 years* since I had some!"

I burst out into a fit of laughter at her reference. Harmony has always been inclined to over exaggerate things and this is no different.

"So then, who do you think should know about our plans?" I wonder aloud prior to continuing, "Your mom?!"

It may seem like such a childish thing to do but I would give anything to have my parents still here. I miss how protected I always felt when they were around and after their passings, I still had Percy. Luckily, Harmony's mom has always made me feel welcomed and protected since high school.

"I was thinking of someone with a little more authority than my mom," she chuckles. "Izzy already knows the plan to meet Rosetta, maybe you could fill her in on when and where we're meeting her just in case."

I'm puzzled because when I think of protective people that are going to ensure we're safe, Izzy isn't the first to come to mind.

"Just because Izzy is a self proclaimed Facebook detective doesn't mean she knows how to keep other people safe," I point out. "And how exactly will telling her ensure our safety?" I question with a bit of sass in my tone because this is our lives we're talking about.

I can hear Harmony scoff on the other end of the phone, "I told you she works with the police department all the time, right?" She asks, pausing for my response but continuing when it never comes. "Her brother is a police officer so she has access to an officer at all times. I could've sworn I told you that before."

"You probably did, you know how forgetful this pregnancy brain makes me."

"Don't be blaming my niece on your forgetfulness! Your memory has always been horrible," she says quickly. "Whenever you talk to Izzy just let her know what's going on tomorrow or I can tell her if you don't feel comfortable."

I brush that last sentence off immediately, I may be carrying a child but I'm no longer one. I can definitely speak for myself.

"Nah girl, it's cool. I'll tell her when I talk to her again," I eventually say, deciding that Harmony doesn't mean any harm by her suggestion.

I notice Anthony's truck a few cars ahead of me, pulling into an Ace Hardware parking lot. *I wonder what he's getting from there.* He's a man though, so I'm sure he picking up some things for a repair around his apartment. But that strikes me as even weirder because there's usually a maintenance person to make all repairs at apartment complexes. I avert my eyes back to the road as I pass the hardware store and carry on in the direction of my home.

"Okay, cool. Well Imma let you go, I just wanted to see if something seemed off about Ant or if it was just me. I'll get up with you tomorrow before I head over to your house," Harmony says. "Please remember to fill Izzy in when you talk to her."

"I will, I promise. I'll see you tomorrow. Bye." I reply as I disconnect the call and turn on one of my favorite true crime podcasts to listen to for the remainder of my drive home.

Chapter 14

Janelle

Today is the day I finally will get some answers! The sun is out, it's a beautiful September day and I'm anxiously awaiting five o'clock. I feel like I've aged fifty years since finding out Rosetta has some kind of ties to Percy, of course it's likely due to a lack of rest.

This pregnancy has been steadily draining what little energy I have left and it doesn't help that I haven't been able to get much sleep. It's as if my baby girl knows when I'm laying down to rest because she immediately gets active, making it impossible for me to get comfortable.

I'm not sure how women all over the world are able to handle multiple pregnancies alone. I definitely have a newfound appreciation for women that are alone throughout their pregnancies. *I can't imagine how difficult life is about to become after I give birth.*

I throw back the comforter on my bed, scooting out and rushing to the bathroom, praying silently to myself that I don't pee on myself before reaching the toilet. Luckily, I made it in time. It's insane the amount of pressure a growing baby puts on your bladder.

Continuing with my morning routine, I hop in the shower and brush my teeth afterwards to prepare for my day.

I throw a chamomile tea K-cup and some water into my Keurig, then place my mug underneath the water outlet to prepare some tea for myself before stepping out onto my front porch.

I take a seat in my old school styled white rocking chair and take a moment to live in the moment. Today may be the last day of life as I know it, depending on what I find out from Rosetta. This life, my life, may have all been a lie.

I relish in the moment, taking a moment to say a prayer out loud while crossing my fingers that my message reaches all the way to Heaven.

Dear Lord, I've strayed so far away from you that I'm not even sure if you can still hear me but if you can, thank you for hearing my cries. Please keep us safe during our journey to find out the truth with Rosetta. In Jesus Christ's name I pray, amen.

I sip on my tea as I soak in the beauty of the nature surrounding my house. I begin to reminisce on my childhood, sitting out on the porch with my mom and dad during the early days of fall before the school year started. They always had a cup of coffee while I had my tea. The memory brings tears to my eyes when I recall my dad teaching me unique facts about the birds we'd see stop by the birdhouse that he helped me build.

My phone dings, pulling my thoughts back to the present. I grab it to unlock with my face, seeing a message from Izzy.

Hi Janelle, are you available for a call real quick? It won't take long.

I consider saying no so that I can sit and enjoy nature for a bit longer but also to avoid any further unwanted communication from Percy but I remember I need to tell her our plans to meet with Rosetta later today.

Hey! Yeah, that's fine. I need to fill you in on something real quick myself.

Moments later, my phone rings.

"Hello?"

"Janelle.. Hi! I just wanted to chat real quickly. So, you remember how I told you about Rosetta's son?" She pauses after that question for just a beat, speaking quickly in Spanish to someone on her end, then continues without giving me a chance to answer. "Well, it's the strangest thing. I can't find *any* information on him aside from his name, this leads me to believe that he wasn't her biological son."

This is why I like Izzy, she gives it to me straight. She doesn't waste time beating around the bush but instead gets directly to the point.

"Ahh..." I say in acknowledgment but not really understanding why I need to know this information. "So what does this mean? Does your search for more information about him end here?" I ask her, suddenly remembering to update her on meeting up with Rosetta. "Actually... I guess it doesn't really matter since Harmony, Anthony and I are going out to her place later today at five. I can ask her about him if everything goes well."

I say this in a much chipper voice than I truly feel. I'm honestly just ready to hear her explanation about the meet ups with Percy, I have no desire to learn about her personal life.

"Oh?" says Izzy, clearly surprised by this information. "So I take it you and Anthony are okay with each other now?"

How exactly should I phrase this? Because although me and Ant are cool with one another, I'm not fully letting my guard down with him.

"Good, so you realized that Anthony is the "coworker" I was telling you about at the restaurant?" I chuckle softly.

"Yeah, I figured. But did I hear you right? Y'all are going to her house? Are you sure that's a good idea?" She asks with concern.

"I know, I know. Trust me, her house was not my first choice." I say. "But she is a convicted felon, out on parole and isn't allowed to go anywhere for real. So we decided that her house would be easiest."

"I see," she says, although I can tell from the way she says it that there's more she wants to say.

"It's fine though. She may be a convicted felon but we'll have Anthony with us. He can handle things if she gets out of hand."

Even as I say this, speaking with more confidence than I actually feel, I know I'm not fooling anyone. My mind has been racing with thoughts of scenarios that may go left. What if we get there and she wants to take my baby or something like in those Lifetime movies my mom used to watch and cry over? I mean she was a kidnapper, who's to say that prison truly changed her?

"If you say so. By the way, how well do you know Anthony?" She asks.

"I've known him for a few months. He worked with my husband at FCI Fairfield briefly before his wreck, he was fairly new when Percy passed." I explain to Izzy as I grab my cup and step back inside.

"So not very well, huh?" She questions in a way that makes my anxiety skyrocket.

"Nah, not really. But Harmony's cousin has known him for a few years and says he's one of the good ones."

"I can't for the life of me understand why but I can't shake the feeling that there's something untruthful about him," she says with trepidation. "The darkness that came over me when I saw him on FaceTime yesterday was unsettling to the point I don't think you should be alone with him." Izzy hesitates before continuing, "You nor Harmony. Do you know his background, where he grew up? Anything?"

I'm embarrassed to admit that I've never even thought to ask about his childhood but it couldn't have been too rough since he turned out okay. I was so overwhelmed with grief that I didn't bother learning his history. Plus, Harmony knew of him from her cousin so he's got to be a decent guy, I convince myself.

"Umm... Well, no. I don't really know much about him," I reply unsure of what Izzy is really trying to tell me. "Why? Do you think he's dangerous?"

Izzy doesn't immediately answer which results in me anxiously pacing back and forth from my living room to the kitchen.

"I don't want to say that because I don't know this man but I know that type of darkness I felt when I saw him on that call. The energy that a person puts out is usually very evident to me, instantly my head starts pounding and I feel nauseous."

If there's one thing I know about evil people and their energy is that any signs of discomfort and distress signifies negative energy.

Izzy continues, "I just want you two to be careful around him. Some people are experts at hiding who they truly are. And I just can't help but think of Percy's message to you."

I pull a chair out from under my kitchen table to rest from all the pacing I've done. I'm at the point in my pregnancy where it hurts to do just about anything.

"I'll keep that in mind, but I better get going. I've got to get dressed and ready to meet Rosetta. We'll be fine." I reassure her before saying bye and disconnecting the call.

Chapter 15

Janelle

I glance at my watch for the time before hearing Alexa announce "Someone is at your door." *Finally!* I think to myself, today has been a drag with time moving as slow as molasses.

I grab my purse before opening the door and heading out. Anthony greets me with a smile and walks me towards the passenger side of my truck. Harmony has pulled onto my grass, next to where Anthony's truck is parked, walking towards us.

"You ready to get some answers?" She asks as she opens the back car door and climbs in.

Anthony opens the door for me as I proceed to balance myself on the sidebar to get in. I adjust myself so that I'm seated comfortably with the seat belt stretched to fit over my belly.

"Been ready." I answer, determined to be okay with whatever I find out today.

Most of the ride is filled with karaoke performances by me and Harmony, many of which were Grammy worthy. We arrive in Howie with about twenty minutes to kill but decide to head to Rosetta's place anyway.

We turn off of the main road onto a long dirt road that leads us to a large, beautiful brick home with one of those wrap-around porches that my grandparents used to have, sitting on acres of land. Behind the house, slightly to the left is what appears to be a barn. Cows are off to the right, eating grass with hogs on the other side of them.

"*This* is where Rosetta lives?!" I exclaim in wonder. "She's living better than I am!

I'm a bit beside myself because she must have some type of connection for her to be fresh out of prison and now living in this nice ass place.

The closer we get to the house, the more my anxiety increases. Once the truck crawls to a stop in Rosetta's driveway, we jump out, walking towards the massive front door. I step forward to ring the doorbell with Harmony and Anthony standing slightly behind me.

A woman that appears to be around my age opens the heavy wooden door. She has a beautiful dark complexion with coily hair that I know all too well probably stretches to her shoulders when straightened.

She looks surprised by our visit as she says "Hello, who are you and how can I help ya?"

I clear my throat, hoping this is the correct house, "Hi, I'm Janelle Williams. I'm here to speak with Rosetta Hamilton."

Her expression softens "Ah! Yes, Ros did tell me she would be expecting someone today, it must've slipped my mind."

She steps out, closing the door behind her with a purse strapped along her shoulder. I notice Anthony eyeing her curiously but I don't blame him, she has a very nice shape to her.

"Ros is out back, just on the opposite side of the barn. There's a storage shed that I've had converted into a 'she-shed' for her. It's on the back side of the barn, you can't miss it."

We all turn to look in the direction of the barn but are unable to see anything due to the barn's massive size.

"Is it... safe to go back there alone? None of us really know her." I ask the woman with hesitation before quickly side eyeing Harmony and Anthony, hoping my question doesn't come off to her as insensitive.

"Ros wouldn't hurt a fly, she might kidnap one though," answers the woman casually while walking down the steps as we follow. "I'll take you back there, I need to let Ros know I'm running to town anyway."

Harmony, Anthony and I tread alongside the woman down a dirt path leading towards the shed. As we get closer to the barn I start to hear horses in stables neighing.

Just like she said, the shed is on the back side of the barn. It appears much larger than a normal storage shed. It has a single window on the side with a plain white door for the entrance. The woman knocks on the door and seconds later an older woman with gray hair plaited back into two braids opens the door. She eyes each one of us up and down, pausing slightly when her eyes land on Anthony, before she speaks.

"Hi, you must be Janelle," she says as she extends a hand.

"Hello, you would be correct." I turn slightly to introduce Harmony since she already knows Anthony from prison. "This is my best friend, Harmony."

Harmony lifts a hand and waves while saying "Hi, it's nice to meet you."

"Well, go ahead and invite them in, Ros," says the woman. "I was just on my way to town to run a few errands, do you need anything?"

"Oh, yes. Yes, come in please and no, I don't. Thank you for asking" answers Rosetta once she finally peels her eyes off of me.

I'm a bit uncomfortable with the way she's staring at me, I'm not sure how to perceive her.

The woman nods her head and starts to walk back towards her house.

One by one, we follow each other into her place. I must admit she has the place decorated nicely with bright mustard yellow walls and a single cocoa brown sofa with burnt orange throw pillows that has different geometric shapes. Across from the living room is a small kitchen area with a single sink and a mini stove that has only three eyes. There is a small wooden table with two chairs in one corner of the shed and in the opposite corner lies her bed. It's a small, full sized bed with a bright sunflower blanket that has fringes along the edges.

"You can have a seat on the sofa, I'll grab a chair. Would y'all like a glass of water?" Rosetta asks as she reaches for a chair from her table.

"No, thanks." I answer politely while Harmony and Anthony follow suit.

Rosetta smiles at me as she takes a seat, "So... where would you like to start?"

Harmony reaches over, gently giving my hand a squeeze before I can reply. This small gesture seems to do wonders to calm the nervousness I'm feeling.

"I guess from the beginning," I say in one quick breath. "How did you know my husband, Percy?"

"Well, Hunny. I knew him from prison." She says as if it's the most obvious thing she's ever said.

"Okay, you were texting him... Why? How long had that been going on?"

She shifts uncomfortably in her seat, dropping her head before answering.

"Not very long, all I wanted was for him to tell you about me."

Instantly, my face I feel a fit of rage crawling its way throughout my body. It's as if the walls of this room are closing in on me and it's getting difficult to breathe. I realize what she says from this point on may be heart wrenching to hear.

Harmony obviously notices the shift in me because she asks if I need to get some air.

"Would you like to step outside?" asks Rosetta standing and waving her arm towards the door we just entered.

"Yes, I would like that," I answer as I stand, racing towards the door.

Harmony is the first one out behind me, she rushes towards me, placing a soft hand on my back.

"Nelle, are you ready for this conversation?" She questions eyeing me carefully.

I take a few deep breaths to settle nausea threatening to escape my body before replying "I just needed some air."

"Okay, well we're gonna give you two some privacy. We'll be just over here near the cows" she says as she points towards the fence enclosing the cows.

I nod my head and turn back towards the door where I see Anthony and Rosetta appear. Harmony motions for Anthony to follow her while I turn my attention back to Rosetta.

"I'm sorry. This is a bit difficult to hear." I explain before continuing, "So y'all were together?" I question, fearful of her response.

"Yes, we were together that unfortunate day. I escaped from the truck because I was afraid I'd be blamed for his wreck and thrown back in prison."

"So you left the man you were having an affair with, to die all alone?" I spit out with disgust. "How could you do that? Did his life mean nothing to you?!"

Confusion overcomes Rosetta's face as she stands there open mouthed and blinking abnormally fast.

"You think..." she begins then pauses for a moment before going on, "You think I had an *affair* with your husband!?"

A smirk lines the corners of her mouth as she attempts to stifle her laughter with no success.

Pure rage fills me, as I scowl at her "Isn't that what the hell I just asked you?!"

That must have come out louder than I expected because I feel Anthony and Harmony look over at us.

Rosetta waves them off and replies "No, you asked if I was with your husband, baby. And I said yes, I was in the vehicle with him during that dreadful day."

It's my turn to be confused. If they weren't having an affair, what were they doing together?

"So you weren't having an affair with Percy?" I ask in befuddlement as I rub a hand across my belly.

Rosetta smiles and ushers me towards the barn. I take a glance back towards Harmony and Anthony and figure they're close enough to get to me if Rosetta tries to harm me while inside.

"Come with me while I tend to my duties and explain everything from the beginning," she says as she opens the ginormous sliding barn door and I follow her inside.

Chapter 16

Anthony

I can tell Janelle is puzzled by the blank expression on her face as I hear Rosetta open the barn door.

I'll have to be fairly quick to get Janelle all to myself. I think to myself as I turn back to figure out the plan to get rid of Harmony.

"Hey Rosetta, could I use your bathroom?" asks Harmony just before Rosetta and Janelle disappear into the barn.

Rosetta turns back towards us and says "Sure baby. It's around the side of the shed. It's connected to the opposite side of the wall where the kitchen sink is," before entering the building.

Lady luck must be on my side today.

I stay behind along the wooden fence where the cows pasture begins while Harmony walks towards the bathroom. I pet one of the cows until all three women are no longer in sight then quickly run to my truck, pulling out the rope I threw into the back of the pickup. I throw the coiled rope over my shoulder and race to the back of the shed before Harmony has time to exit the bathroom.

I'm damn near out of breath just as Harmony opens the door to leave.

"Oh. You didn't have to wait here for me," she says with surprise on her face.

I stand directly in front of her, preventing her from exiting as my face takes on a sinister grin.

"I'm not the one that'll be doing the waiting." I say with a menacing laugh.

Perplexed, Harmony opens her mouth to say something but doesn't have time to speak, as my fist connects to her face. She doesn't have time to see it coming before she's whimpering on the bathroom floor with blood pouring from her nose. Immediately, pain is radiating from my hand but the rush of adrenaline consumes me.

Harmony is down and disoriented but still awake. It's a pleasure to see her in pain, I step inside, gripping her under the arms to pull her body back into the bathroom completely.

She curls up on the floor, moaning a bit too loud for my liking as I step over her, squatting down so that we're eye level.

"Shut your fucking mouth or I *will* kill you." I spit out with a coldness that could freeze a hot tub.

CHAPTER 16

Harmony's eyes grow wide as the realization that Rosetta isn't the one they should be afraid of sets in.

She starts screaming but quickly falls silent after another blow directly to the face. The top half of her body falls back with a loud thump as I climb over her, giving her a few more smacks to the face to make sure she's knocked out.

She doesn't move, I stand and use the bottom of my boots to roll her onto her stomach. Next, I take the rope from my shoulder and proceed to tie Harmony's arms behind her back and her feet together.

I have to work quickly to get her loaded onto my shoulder and into the back of my truck. *Dammit man! She's heavier than she looks.*

By the time I'm halfway to my truck, I decide it may be easier to pull her body along the grass that lies on the edge of the dirt path instead.

I hurl Harmony, belly side down, into the backseat of my pickup, knocking her head carelessly against the headrest. Closing the door, I ensure all windows are up and doors are locked.

She'll wake up after while, but this should stall her until I have what I want.

Chapter 17

Janelle

The smell of shit hits me as soon as we step inside the barn, it'll take a few minutes before my nose adjusts to the scent.

Rosetta steps into one of the stables to love on one of the horses. It's a gorgeous, golden brown color with a long, silky mane and full tail.

"This is Spirit." She says as I gaze at the beautiful creature from afar. "Tending to animals seems to give me a reason to live," she explains.

I nod in understanding, "So... I'm here for answers. What did you want Percy to tell me?"

She lets out an exasperated breath and steps outside the stable. "I wanted you to know the truth."

"And what is the truth?" I ask with my arms now crossed in front of my chest.

"I kidnapped your sister," Rosetta blurts out quickly.

Her response catches me off guard but I laugh it off as I instantly recall people saying she is crazy.

"You've got the wrong person, lady!" I manage to get out in between chuckles. "I'm an only child, just as my mom and dad were."

Rosetta starts to pace, shaking her head from side to side in disagreement. "No, no, no," she says. "That's the reason I went to prison, it was because I took her! I, I..., I kidnapped her! She was your twin sister. I mean, dammit! You look just like her! "

I'm stunned and not sure what to say. She seems so sure of herself but then again, crazy people are notorious for appearing normal. *But I'm also worried that if I disagree with her again, could it upset her to the point of her becoming violent? I've got to make her realize she's wrong. But how?*

"Rosetta, I'm really sorry but I do not have any siblings," I reply . "But even if I did, what does that have to do with my husband?"

"Shut up, child, I'm not done speaking," she spits out, irritation filling the air.

I immediately turn to leave in order to keep from disrespecting an elder (because who does she think she is speaking to like that) but pause and turn back to Rosetta before saying "If you can't tell me what I need to know regarding my husband, then I guess this was all for nothing."

I wait for a response that never comes so I guide myself out. Just before reaching the door Rosetta stops me.

"Wait a minute, okay!? Just wait a damn minute," she fires out, as she rushes to stop me from sliding the massive door open. "This is why I wanted Percy to tell you, I knew you wouldn't believe me. He knew the truth although like you, he didn't believe me at first either."

I stand there dumbfounded with a blank expression on my face. *Could she be telling the truth?*

"What the hell do you mean he didn't believe you at first? What was it that changed his mind?" I question with bewilderment in my voice. "Would you just spit it out!?"

Rosetta's eyes quickly darts from me back to Spirit the horse.

"When I was younger, I was pregnant with twins, a girl and a boy," says Rosetta as tears begin to pool in her eyes. "One day I started bleeding and having contractions while I was at work, they rushed me to the hospital. Being pregnant with twins, I knew early labor could spontaneously happen but still, I hoped for the best."

"Could you just get to the point, Rosetta? I don't need your whole life story." I snarl at her with impatience spilling from every word.

"Long story short, I ended up giving birth to my twins but the following day, my daughter took her final breath." Rosetta rushes out, finally allowing her tears to fully form and spill from her eyes. "I was devastated. I loved my boys but I was finally getting my 'mini-me'" she cries out hopelessly. "But that was all snatched away from me before she even reached this earth side."

Slowly, the pieces of the puzzle are finally falling in place. I see where this is going but how am I to know it's the truth?

"Your mother, God bless her soul, just so happened to be pregnant with twins and in labor at the same time I was. We actually shared a single room with a curtain dividing our beds. Back in the 80's, it was easy to steal newborns from hospitals. Most of the nurses didn't half way care about those newborns no how, especially little black babies," she continues, regret filling her eyes.

"So you switched your dead baby for my twin sister?" I conclude in barely a whisper, as my throat dries, making it difficult to swallow.

Rosetta pauses allowing me to collect my thoughts and finally say something but continues when I'm unable to find any words. "I never meant to hurt anyone but I wasn't thinking clearly. I can't imagine how your parents felt when it first happened. I wish I could apologize to them, especially your mother."

"DON'T. Don't you dare mention my mother. You want me to believe that I had a twin sister I knew nothing about? And you expect me to believe you, a convicted felon and known kidnapper, over my parents?" I throw out still in disbelief of what Rosetta is explaining to me. "What sense does that make? It doesn't. I'm done here."

Before I can walk off, Rosetta hurries over to a small, round three legged rusting, metal table with a small photo album setting on it. She picks it up and practically jogs back over to me, placing the album in my hands.

"Look at these, tell me what you see…" she trails off.

I take the book from her, flipping open the first few pages. It's filled with photos of a younger me except, it's not me. I don't recognize any of the people or backgrounds in these photos.

"This…" I say pausing slightly to allow my brain enough time to completely form the rest of my sentence. "This is my sister?" I ask, too stunned to get anything more out.

"Yes, baby. That's what I've been trying to tell you. This was your twin sister, Chanelle. Desperate to bring home my baby girl, I took her and passed her off as my own, leaving your mother devastated."

Unsure how to respond, I allow myself time to process everything. *What. The. Fuck!*

My heart is racing a mile a minute, I feel lightheaded and my vision starts to tunnel. *Air… I need fresh air.*

Turning away to leave, I muster up enough effort to slide the heavy barn door open just enough to fit through it. But I'm stopped short as I nearly collide into Anthony with what appears to be blood staining his shirt.

Chapter 18

Anthony

B efore I can lift my arms up to open the door, it recedes with a disheveled Janelle rushing out.

For once, relief resolves on her face at the sight of me. This is everything I've ever wanted, just for someone to actually see me.

"What's wrong? Did she hurt you?" I ask, barging my way in towards Rosetta, my biggest concern being Janelle.

Janelle grabs my arm, pulling me back while she cries out "I don't know what the fuck to believe! This was a mistake!"

I wrap a hysterical Janelle in a close yet brief embrace before turning towards Rosetta with a wicked smile, "Is that right…. Mama Ros?"

With that simple phrase, Rosetta's eyes darken and she gasps, catching her breath as she realizes my true identity.

"Janelle, get away from him!", she shouts loudly. "He's not who you think he is!"

Janelle's eyes bounce from me to Rosetta and back to me again. No longer sure what to believe, she looks for another way out but quickly changes her mind, seeing there's only one way in and out.

I give a quick, charming grin, "Do you really think she's going to believe *you* over me?" I chuckle in amusement, "You are the thief, the felon… the murderer."

"A murderer?!" Janelle asks incredulously, pulling back from me, holding her hands to her head then she shakes it.

I give her a smirk and throw my hands up, "What can I say? Murderers must run in the family." I peer back over to Rosetta continuing, "Isn't that right, Mama Ros?"

Rosetta dashes towards Janelle in what I can only assume is an effort to distance her from me but she freezes inches from me as she spots the gun in my hand.

Janelle shrieks, "Stop! Please!"

Rosetta throws her hands up as if that'll keep me from pulling the trigger, pleading for me to think about my actions.

"Don't do this, baby. Just put the gun down, no one here has to get hurt."

Feeling ridiculed, I spit out "No one has to get hurt?" I struggle to compose myself, "Yet I've suffered silently from you. I was the one you

136

birthed, yet you treated me like shit!"

With pleading eyes, Rosetta responds with "I know baby,I am so very sorry but I'm out now, allow me to make that up to you."

Janelle's head bounces from me to Rosetta as her stupid, entitled mind struggles to catch up.

Rosetta slowly steps between Janelle and I with her palms still facing the sky. "Janelle doesn't have anything to do with this, it is *me* you're upset with. Let her go, I'm the one you're angry at."

She's right, this has nothing to do with Janelle, aside from the fact that she's the identical twin sister of my fake sister. The one whom I despised for getting all of Mama Ros's attention.

"She has everything to do with this!" I bark hatefully. "She has the same face as the girl I hated the most! I loved you so much and all I ever wanted was to feel the same from you in return."

My eyes start to sting as I manage to blink away tears that are forming in the lower part of my eyes.

"DeMetrius, listen to me, love. I loved you and your siblings all the sa-."

"LIE TO ME AGAIN, DAMMIT!" I roar, pacing back and forth, gun still drawn with my finger placed carefully on the trigger. "It was always obvious I never mattered to you."

"No! That's not true," shrieks Rosetta with tears steadily streaming down her face. "You were always so self sufficient. I knew you were different from a very young age, always independent. At that time I figured that was a good thing, I didn't have to hover over you constantly. You are my miracle child, you overcame every single obstacle stacked against you as a preemie, my love."

I open my mouth to reply but immediately pause at the sound of someone on the other side of the sliding door. As the door is pulled open, I'm able to recognize the voice as the woman from earlier. I reach for Janelle since she's closest to me, aiming the gun at her head.

"One word from either of you and she dies."

Chapter 19

Janelle

My head is spinning, the coldness of the gun against my forehead sends a shiver down my spine that nearly solidifies the blood coursing through my veins.

This is it, I'm finally gonna be reunited with Percy, I think to myself.

I see Rosetta's mouth moving but I can't make out what she's saying due to the accelerated thumping sound of my own heart, thundering so boisterously in my ears, that it's the only sound I'm able to make sense of.

A thin sliver of light from the setting sun appears along a bale of straw, positioned diagonally across from the door as the woman from earlier pulls it ajar.

"Ros, are you out here? I thought I heard someone scream—" she stops short, confusion, instantly followed by terror filling every crevice of her face as she steps into the barn, observing the sight of us. She tries to turn back but it's too late, Anthony, or DeMetrius, is now pointing his gun towards her.

"How nice of you to join us… Sharon," he hisses in a tone so vile even the devil himself would tremble in fear.

Sharon freezes at the mention of her name as her eyes scan Anthony's face from the top to bottom, searching for some type of recognition.

"H- How do you know my name?" she manages to get out.

Anthony swiftly marches over to pull the barn door closed then escorts Sharon next to me, gun still aimed at her.

"What a shame, what a shame?" He says, shaking his head softly from side to side. "How is it you two have forgotten me so easily, yet you both have lived in my head for years?"

Anthony aims the gun between the three of us before banging it against his head in frustration.

"Ahh!", he shouts, pacing back and forth in frustration. "All I ever wanted was to be seen. DeAndre, the problem child, always into shit he shouldn't have been into while Chanelle was the baby girl you always wanted. But what about me? I yearned to be loved and cared about, too!"

I glance nervously around the area for anything I can use as a weapon as he turns away from me.

"My brother was the only one who understood me!" He stops directly in front of Sharon and lifts a finger pointedly at her, "AND YOU! Because of *you*, always so jealous of DeAndre's sexual attraction to Chanelle, that you cost my brother his life!"

Anthony then turns his attention to Rosetta before continuing, "He was my best friend before Chanelle started going through her womanly changes, growing breasts and maturing in a way we had never seen."

Sharon musters up the courage to speak first. "DeMetrius," she says softly, "I never meant for things to turn out this way. I thought DeAndre would go away and come out rehabilitated as a different person." Tears slowly spill from her face as she continues, "Guilt eats at me every single day because regardless of what you think, I loved him."

Rosetta rubs Sharon's back as she continues to sob then adds in a voice filled with sorrow, "I should have believed you. DeAndre should have been a protector to you and Chanelle, instead you two needed protection from him," she says, closing her eyes and shaking away the thought. "I wasn't ready to accept that but when she died, I lost it. I didn't mean for things to go as far as they did."

Sharon leans into Rosetta's open arms for a short embrace before Anthony, or *perhaps I should say DeMetrius*, interrupts the sentimental moment between the two women.

"OH, GIVE ME A FUCKING BREAK!" He bellows, "And still, no one gives a fuck about me! How is it that I'm the one that was left abandoned, all alone at the age of 13 yet she's the one you're comforting? Unfuckingbelievable!"

DeMetrius rubs his hands over his head in disbelief.

"You don't love me, you've never loved me. I was always just a constant reminder of your real dead daughter, my twin sister." He glares at Rosetta, "You wanted your sweet baby girl more than anything, and you got one apparently forgetting about me in the process. I hated Chanelle for the love and affection she received from you, yet I'm the next of kin you never truly wanted. Why didn't you love me, Ma? Why was I not good enough?"

Finally, I believe I have a clear understanding of how the events of today led here.

Rosetta's oldest son, DeAndre, the problem child, kept the attention of his mom while DeMetrius seemingly lacked love and affection from her as she cared for Chanelle, my kidnapped twin sister.

Before I can process any more, the sound of the barn door sliding open interrupts my thoughts.

This obviously isn't part of the plan from the dumbstruck expression on DeMetrius' face. Simultaneously, we all turn towards the door as we anxiously wait to see who's on the other side.

Chapter 20

Janelle

Time seems to stand still, as seconds tick by without anyone stepping into sight, outside of the barn.

DeMetrius walks towards the exit but quickly halts, probably thinking twice about who could be on the other side.

"You two, up front." He directs Sharon and Rosetta to step over the barn door's threshold, likely in hopes of whoever is out there attacking the women first.

Neither of them moves an inch until he removes the gun from the small of my back and waves it from me to them. Grabbing hold of each other, they timidly inch towards the exit.

Just before stepping out, Rosetta shouts "Don't shoot! We're unarmed!"

As soon as those words have left her lips, DeMetrius pulls me in front of him, guiding me towards the two women with his arm around my neck and the gun placed at the side of my head. He uses my body as his shield as we step out of the barn.

It has to be Harmony! She had to hear Anthony/DeMetrius as loud as he was.

My eyes shift around quickly in search of Harmony, hopeful yet fearful of the gun she said she was bringing.

It's hard to make anything out now that the sun has nearly set. My eyes dart to Rosetta's house but the goose neck-like, solar light fixtures along the side of it are either extremely sensitive to light, observing what remains of daylight, or they do not work.

"Drop the gun!" calls out a vaguely familiar female voice.

DeMetrius flinches, hastily turning in the direction of the voice. I piss myself in response, unintentionally of course.

"Don't make me tell you twice," the female voice calls again. "If you haven't lowered the gun by the time I count to three, I'm shooting."

She sounds younger than Harmony. Where the hell have I heard this voice!?

DeMetrius laughs her threat off, "You don't scare me!"

"One…" counts the girl, "two…"

"Three," comes another woman's voice from the opposite direction, followed by a single gunshot.

I instinctively close my eyes, bracing myself for the onset of a searing flame, piercing my brain while blood leaks from me, similar to that of a waterfall. I expect for everything to turn to dark but when it doesn't, I realize I'm not in any pain either.

I open my eyes cautiously, afraid of what I may see. To my surprise, none of us are hurt.

DeMetrius, now fuming, pushes me over to Rosetta and Sharon as he moves back and forth, pointing his gun in each direction of the women's voices.

"Next time I won't miss," the second voice promises. "No one has to get hurt, just put the gun down and let's talk!"

This voice is familiar as well, the enunciation of her words make me think it's Izzy.

But I don't recall giving her the address to Rosetta's house and where the fuck is Harmony?

DeMetrius turns towards the second voice, focusing hard to make out the dark shadowy figure in the distance.

He must think he can take her down because he walks in her direction slowly, gun still aimed in her path.

Although I'm afraid for the woman's life, I use this opportunity to sneak towards DeMetrius' truck. Unfortunately for me, Rosetta and Sharon decide to follow, drawing his attention back to us.

"Did I say you bitches could leave?" He shouts, turning the gun back on the three of us.

We freeze, too afraid he may pull the trigger to dare take another step.

Finally, the light above Rosetta's house, along with a few other lights surrounding the property, comes on. I take in my surroundings, looking in the direction of the first woman's voice and spot Brandi, the waitress from the restaurant.

What the hell? Why is she here?

"Ahh...what was it, Brandi, correct?" DeMetrius mocks with a devilish grin. He cocks the gun and points it towards her.

Sharon lurches forward in a blur, pushing past me and Rosetta to get to DeMetrius while screaming at the top of her lungs "Noooo!"

DeMetrius glances back to see her running towards him. He turns, firing the gun at Sharon before firing once more in the direction of the second woman's voice. Instantly, I hear groaning from the woman while Sharon simultaneously drops to the ground.

Brandi takes off running in Sharon's direction, saying "Mama! No!" once she made it to Sharon's limp body lying on the ground.

DeMetrius doesn't bother being concerned with either of them but instead directs his attention back to me and Rosetta.

Clinging to each other as we await our demise, Rosetta begins to recite the Lord's Prayer. Although I still sometimes question my faith, I join her in prayer but it has little effect on DeMetrius.

"Oh, Mama Ros... it's no use, your God isn't here to save you," he mocks with narrowing eyes. "I've waited my entire life for a chance to make you pay for the way you treated me, to see this exact fear in your eyes."

"I was a different person back then, baby. Don't do this, it's not too late! I love you, DeMetrius!"

He's getting too close for comfort, so I attempt to slowly distance myself from Rosetta but it isn't quick enough.

"Unfortunately for you, my dear mother, love doesn't live here anymore."

DeMetrius fires a single head shot. Everything seems to go into slow motion as I watch a bullet hole enter Rosetta's skull, instantly feeling her blood and brain matter splatter directly on me. I can't think, I can't feel, I'm in total shock.

Knowing what fate lies ahead if I continue to stand there in my stupor, I turn using every ounce of strength I have left in my jello legs to run towards the truck. I manage to get within about fifteen feet of the vehicle before a series of gunfire explodes behind me.

I feel a small inkling of pain that erupts into the most agonizing pain I've ever known, burst through my back. At once, I see blood pooling from the exit wound in my belly. I fall to my hands and knees but determined to defy my body's instinct to give in to the pain, I continue to inch towards the truck on all fours. Too afraid of the scene I might see, I refuse to look back. Instead, I find myself praying out to God, hoping He remembers me after all these years, to keep me and my baby safe.

It isn't until I make it to the far side of the truck, finally able to lean against the front passenger side wheel that my brain has time to work again. Immediately, I notice the absence of gunfire.

Or maybe this is how it is when a person dies. Hearing goes out first, then sight but dammit! I need this pain to go away.

The shots must have really stopped because I begin to hear banging from inside the truck. I attempt to push myself from the ground but I can't get up, it hurts too bad and I'm too weak.

Just as the banging begins to somewhat fade, I prepare myself for another burst of agony as I lean sideways, peering around the front of the truck.

The sudden movement blurs my vision, making me dizzy, as I feel another trickle of water flow out of me.

Why am I peeing so much?

I take one final glance over in Demetrius's direction, my vision blurs just as I see what I think is a male figure walking towards me.

He's gonna kill me. I think to myself, *At least the pain will stop and I'll be with my family again.*

I accept that this will all soon be over as I lie my head back against the truck's tire. I think the knocking from inside the truck starts again just as the dark figure inches closer towards the truck.

CHAPTER 20

A sense of calmness overtakes me just as the knocking stops, the pain ends and my vision fades to total and complete darkness.

Chapter 21

Janelle - Epilogue

It's been one year since that fateful night in Howie, SC. Honestly, I'm surprised we survived! This journey has been a long and daunting one but I wouldn't change it for the world.

After I lost consciousness that night, I was life-flighted to the Bridgeport Memorial Hospital where my daughter, Journi was born by cesarean section. They have a state of the art NICU that was better suited for Journi. I named her that because this has most definitely been quite the journey!

The bullet I was struck with entered and exited in the most perfect way possible. Half an inch to the left or right and neither me nor my daughter would be here today.

Due to her being a preemie, her health was up and down but she's a fighter. That's for sure! It was hard to see her in the NICU with so many things attached to her little body. If this is her beginning, the world better get ready! The strength she's displayed in the small amount of time that she has been earth side is astounding.

If it weren't for Harmony sending Izzy her iPhone location and telling her to contact the police if she hadn't heard from us, this would be a different story. Izzy was a genuine life saver that day, she figured out that Anthony was really Rosetta's biological adult son, DeMetrius.

Somehow, she figured out that DeMetrius' social security number was linked to an active credit privacy number, or CPN for short, under the identity of Anthony Miller. It wasn't evident to Rosetta because she hadn't seen him since their last encounter, at age 13 when she abandoned him. She probably wasn't even aware he was still living.

After not hearing from Harmony, Izzy and her police officer brother, Carlos Delgado sped to Rosetta's place after figuring out Anthony's true identity. It turned out being Officer Carlos Delgado that I saw walking towards me that late September night, not DeMetrius. Thankfully, he called for back up before they even arrived at Rosetta's.

Due to Sharon's home being on acres of land, Carlos was able to notify the hospital that life-flight services were required for me and they were able to land in a large empty field.

Carlos initiated the rounds of gunfire I heard as I crawled to the side of the truck. DeMetrius left the scene with three bullet wounds in his lower extremities, nothing life threatening. He's now locked away in a maximum security facility, somewhere up north with no chance at parole. I find it kind of ironic how he went from working in a correctional facility to being locked in one for the rest of his life.

Rosetta lived the last few years of her life trying to amend her wrongdoings and dedicated her life to God. That's actually how she got back in contact with Sharon, to apologize for placing blame on Sharon for the chain of events that led to DeAndre's death.

According to Sharon, DeAndre, the problem child began molesting and eventually raping her and Chanelle from the age of 8. Sharon informed Rosetta but of course, her son could do no wrong until Chanelle ended up pregnant. Sharon felt she had no choice but to tell her grandmother what was happening. Chanelle moved in with Sharon and her grandmother for the remainder of her pregnancy until her death during childbirth. At which point, Rosetta completely lost it, killed DeAndre, abandoned DeMetrius and skipped town. It wasn't until Rosetta found God in prison that she started to take accountability for her role in everything that happened.

Sharon began visiting Rosetta in prison one year before she was released. They had both forgiven each other for everything and had been working on mending their complicated relationship. Rosetta had one day hoped to meet her grandchild, Brandi, unfortunately she never got that chance.

Speaking of Brandi, can you imagine the shock I had when I learned that she's my actual, blood-related niece? Now, I finally have the family that I always wanted.

Sharon and Izzy have become just as close friends as Harmony and I. We meet up at least once a week for a girl's day or night, oftentimes at The Chew so that we can leave Brandi enormous tips.

Today, however, we're meeting for a different reason. Journi is turning a year old today and we plan to go all out for it! All three ladies along with Brandi are on their way over at this very second to help us celebrate.

I hear keys jingle in the front door before Carl walks in, setting the large cake in his hands on an end table. He walks over to the high chair that's holding Journi as she squeals, begging him to pick her up.

"Hey Jour, Jour!" He says, lifting her to kiss her chubby, little cheek.

My heart is finally bursting with pure happiness as I realize the family I've made with Journi, Harmony, Brandi and our new friends, is the family I've always wanted.

After we open presents, I'm taking Journi to visit her dad's grave. She will always know who he was to her as long as her family is around. I'm sure I'll even tell her about Rosetta and her Aunt Chanelle one day.

The ladies arrive together as I open the door, letting them in. They give a quick greeting but make their way to the birthday girl, who's still squealing and jumping with delight.

The sight reminds me of an old African Proverb my dad used to quote, *A family is like a tree, it can bend but it cannot break.*

About the Author

Krista, an avid, reader since childhood, has always dreamed of writing her own books. In 2022, she successfully accomplished that with the release of her debut children's book titled, "I'm Not Difficult... You Just Don't Understand", a story about life with Sensory Processing Disorder. She is a single mom of three amazing children and previously operated a craft business, KJB Kreations, in Southeast Alabama. Today, she enjoys spending time making memories with close family and friends.

You can connect with me on:
- https://www.kristabeckwithbooks.com
- https://www.facebook.com/everybodyh8krys
- https://www.instagram.com/everybodyh8krys
- https://www.tiktok.com/@everybodyh8krys

Also by Krista Beckwith

I'm Not Difficult... You Just Don't Understand

Sensory Processing Disorder can be hard for anyone to deal with but that doesn't mean it makes you difficult. A little extra understanding and love is all that's needed while learning how to manage life with it.